A Convenient Engagement

Brides of Brighton Book 1

ASHTYN NEWBOLD

ISBN 13: 9781075315084

Front cover design by Blue Water Books

For Mom and Dad, who believed I could.

Chapter 1

ENGLAND, SUMMER, 1813

Sunlight came even more rarely than silence through Amelia Buxton's second story window. It was not often that the two came together. But despite the hustle of carriages and neighbors beneath her, Amelia breathed a sigh of contentment as the sweet honey rays of the sun soaked into her cheeks through the glass.

"Amelia," The voice of her father hung in the doorway, making her jump. More rare than silence or sunshine each morning was the absence of that disapproving salutation from her father.

"Good morning, Papa." Amelia forced a smile, wiping away the perspiration from her palms. Mr. Buxton was not an intimidating man when one observed him in passing. With a slight frame, pale eyes, and neat hair, he appeared every bit the charming town gentleman. But when one dared a closer look, they were bound to find the frustration in his gaze, the snap of his lack of patience, and an utter disregard for his daughter's happiness.

Mr. Buxton took another step through the doorway, raising his right eyebrow at Amelia. In all the features of her father's face, Amelia had come to learn that his eyebrows held the most expression. The right eyebrow had always been the one of pending censure.

"My sister has been rambling on about Brighton," he said. "I told you never to speak of your nonsense again."

Oh, yes. *Her nonsense.* The cure of the Brighton waters was far too famous to be claimed solely by Amelia. The Prince Regent himself had taken the cure, luring thousands to Brighton to experience it for themselves. Amelia swallowed as her arms erupted in gooseflesh. The very thought of Brighton, of escaping the over-crowded, smelly boredom of Nottingham set her heart racing. To be so near the ocean? To step in those legendary waters? It was a dream she had been clinging to for years. And now her Aunt Margaret had moved to Nottingham to live with Amelia and her family. Unmarried, joyous, and free, Aunt Margaret held a spirit Amelia wished upon herself. To spend the summer in Brighton with her aunt would be the diversion she had been craving.

Aunt Margaret had suffered from a poor leg since childhood, always carrying a cane. In a casual conversation with her aunt, Amelia had mentioned the cure of the Brighton waters—the legendary idea that one could recover from any ailment by bathing in the waters daily, even drinking of them. But it was only a myth, of course, and if Amelia had noticed the extreme fascination in her aunt's eyes she would have stopped immediately. It did little good to raise the hopes of such a desperate woman.

Twisting her hands in her lap, Amelia scrunched her

brow in false confusion. "Have you not read such reports in the papers? Perhaps that is what spurred Aunt Margaret's fascination with Brighton."

"I know exactly what spurred her fascination with Brighton, and it was certainly not the papers." The color in her father's cheeks deepened with anger. "You are never to give her such absurd ideas again, do you understand?"

"I understand." Amelia avoided his eyes. She wanted to say more, but held her breath.

Aunt Margaret had not stopped speaking of Brighton since the first day Amelia had mentioned it to her, telling Amelia's father that she planned to travel there herself. Aunt Margaret was a very independent woman, unmarried at the age of fifty-two, but with the decline of her health, her brother did not trust that she could live and travel alone. Amelia had to force herself to hold her tongue each time her father rebuked her over her conversations with Aunt Margaret.

Her father adjusted his cravat before clearing his throat. "I cannot have you wasting your time on such frivolous matters. As you know, we are receiving Mr. Clinton for dinner this evening. I do hope you continue to impress him. He was quite taken with you on his last visit but we cannot rely solely on that. I expect he has an offer of marriage on his mind for you."

Amelia tried to hide her revulsion. Mr. Clinton was nearly twice her age and carried a cane. She had never seen the appeal of a dandified man putting on ridiculous airs. "But Papa . . . you must know, I was far from impressed with him."

His face tightened once again. "That does not matter. You have had a fair pick of men, and it is time you decided on one. If your mother were here she might have aligned these things for you, but that is now my responsibility. I do not have much to give you, Amelia. You will need a husband to look after you. I am growing older every day."

Amelia studied his face and the harsh lines that marked it. Since the day her mother had died six years ago, her father had changed. He had grown even colder and even more aloof. The change hadn't been all at once, but little by little, much like the cloud that was passing over the sun. Amelia glanced out the window as the sky grew darker.

He and her mother had never been in love. Amelia had seen the pain it had brought to both their hearts. Hers too. Amelia secretly hoped to have a fate like her aunt's, for she did not need a man at her side to find joy in life. Amelia had watched as her mother found much more trouble than a husband was worth. But Amelia could not entirely discount the marriage. She had been born of it, after all.

"We are all growing older, Papa," she said.

"Precisely. And you need to marry before you become a spinster like Margaret, lonely and pining after an absurd, fabricated cure. You have made your bows in society, and you are lacking nothing that could make you a proper match. It is only your own desires and priorities that must be changed."

Amelia puffed out a breath. That she was *lacking nothing* that could make her a proper match was more absurd than the rumored cure. Brown hair was all the rage yet hers was blonde and straight. Her eyes were a one-dimensional brown, not even with a single fleck of gold to bring a unique quality to them. Her efforts to play the pianoforte were quite novice, and her embroidery appeared to have been stitched by a blind woman—no, a blind child.

A blind child without hands. She chewed her lip to keep herself from delivering her list of inadequacies to her father. It would not help the argument she was about to make.

"How confident are you in my ability to secure a marriage?" she blurted.

Her father crossed his arms, one eyebrow raising up again. It was his left eyebrow this time—the one reserved for inquisition. "As I just professed to you, very confident, should you set your mind to it."

She stood from her chair by the window, taking two careful steps toward him. The idea she was about to propose could be catastrophic . . . or very effective. There was simply no way of knowing beforehand.

"You have said it before, that the men of Nottingham are rather dull and unrefined."

"Indeed."

"Including Mr. Clinton, might I add."

Her father opened his mouth to rebuke her, but seemed to change his mind, conceding with a nod.

Amelia took a deep breath, taking a handful of fabric from her lavender muslin skirts. "It seems to me that you have two problems that need solving. You have a sister who is rather obsessed with the Brighton waters, and a daughter one and twenty who you need married off. Brighton has expanded in recent years, and is home to many eligible gentlemen. There is ample opportunity to be immersed in respectable society. If I were to travel there with Aunt Margaret, we could keep a careful watch on one other, and she will realize the waters hold no cure so her obsession will end. As for me, I will have many opportunities to meet potential suitors."

Her father's jaw twitched and his eyes narrowed. She

could almost see his mind spinning, working through the advantages and disadvantages of the idea. He had not immediately rejected her proposed arrangement. *Perhaps there was hope.*

No, Amelia didn't plan to travel to Brighton with the intent to marry. In fact, there was little about marriage that attracted her at all. Women like Aunt Margaret were free and independent. They did not need the arm of a man to hold onto in order to live a happy life. In truth, Amelia wished to avoid the role of dutiful wife for as long as possible. She had never been witnessed a joyful marriage. But for the sake of earning her father's approval of the trip, she needed to convince him of her devotion to husband hunting.

He had been silent for so long Amelia began to wonder if he had heard her at all.

"How could I be sure of your efforts?" he asked finally.

"Aunt Margaret," she stammered. "Aunt Margaret will be sure to report to you of all my acquaintances, flirtations, and every whit of attention I receive."

Her father rubbed his narrow jaw. "I do not entirely trust her observations. Her memory is not what it used to be, as you know."

"Indeed . . . perhaps you might prompt her to keep a journal of my sociality. A sort of . . . day to day record of my progress with the gentlemen I come to know." Of course Amelia would simply guide Aunt Margaret in writing these entries. Her aunt would be so pleased to be in Brighton that she wouldn't recognize the deceit for a moment.

"That will not work," her father said. "You could very well be formulating false scenarios for her to send to me, just as if you were writing them yourself."

Drat. Her father knew her too well.

"What gives you the idea that I should be so dishonest?" she asked.

"Because I know how little you desire to marry. You have declared your feelings on the matter many times."

Amelia's ears burned. "Perhaps I have experienced a change of heart."

"A heart as stubborn as yours does not change in a day, my dear."

This had begun as Amelia's game, yet her father seemed to be winning. She tried her best not to let desperation enter her voice. "It is not that I don't wish to marry *any man*, Papa. It is only the sort of gentlemen you have chosen for me."

"Oh? And what sort are they?" His voice had hardened.

She sighed in exasperation. "The sort like Mr. Clinton. Dull, quiet, stern. I am not opposed to marriage, only to a marriage that is going to make my life dull and quiet."

"Not all the men I have introduced you to are as such. Mr. Roberts was quite lively and exotic, and very agreeable. He was not dull and quiet at all."

"Yes, but he was too much the contrary. There is a sort of man that lies between Clinton and Roberts. A man that is entertaining and kind, as well as intelligent—but not to the point of boasting. I do not tolerate boasting. He also must be friendly, but not to the point of desperation for attention, like Mr. Roberts." She stopped, noticing the exasperation in her father's features.

"What makes you so certain you will find such a man in Brighton of all places? I have tried for years. I even sent you to London for a season and you returned without a single prospect. You may not like it, but you must settle for a man eventually, even if he falls short of your expectations."

He did not understand. Amelia puffed out another breath of frustration. "Of course, because that is what made you and Mama so very happy."

Silence fell in the air as her father's face deepened yet another shade of crimson. She swallowed. Had she spoken too plainly? It was a weakness of hers. But it was true; her parents had never shared a smile or a kind word that Amelia had witnessed. They tolerated one another, and when her mother had passed away, it was as if her father had seen it as a sort of freedom. All the responsibilities that had been hers were now his. And he reveled in them. It was as if he were certain he performed them better than she ever could have.

Amelia begged to differ. At least Mama had known what made a man handsome.

Amelia's father set his jaw. "You are not going to Brighton." His voice was final, and Amelia felt her heart sink.

"Papa! Please."

"You will gain nothing from the trip besides an increased wayward imagination and a longer list of the unacceptable characteristics of men." Her father turned toward the door, grasping the handle.

"I will gain something from the trip," she blurted without thinking. "I will return engaged."

Her father froze, turning his head over his shoulder to study her.

Her heart hammered in her chest. "You have my word. If you are so certain that it is only my own reluctance to marry that is preventing an engagement, then it should not be very difficult. If you allow me this trip with Aunt Margaret, I will return engaged." She held her breath. What had she done?

Her father's expression lifted slightly. "And what if you fail to deliver on that promise?"

"Pardon?"

"If you fail to return engaged, what then?"

She scowled. "Are you asking me to choose my punishment?"

"Make it a steep one, my dear, for nothing short of that will work."

Amelia's mind raced in search of a suitable idea. "If I do not return engaged . . . I will comb the horses for a month." Her father knew how much she despised stable chores.

He shook his head. "That is far too simple."

"I will . . . consider . . . furthering my acquaintance with the men of Nottingham."

"Unspecific."

"Very well, I will consider furthering my acquaintance with Mr. Clinton." She nearly choked on the name.

Her father paused, deep thought evident in his features. "You will agree to marry Mr. Clinton, should he make the offer he has already suggested to me."

Her heart stopped. "What?"

"Those are my terms. Should you accept this arrangement, I will be quite glad to send you to Brighton with Margaret." Her father smiled, a nefarious grin that Amelia had never before seen on her father's face. How dare he suggest such a thing? She inspected his expression one last time. Unfortunately he did not appear to be jesting.

"Marry Mr. Clinton?" Amelia snorted back a laugh of disbelief. "You would force me into such a marriage?"

"It is fair, is it not? Over the course of the next quarter year, you will have the opportunity to find a better alternative that suits your... taste. It brings a fair amount of urgency to our arrangement." He stepped toward her, giving her upper arm an affectionate squeeze. "I should expect a correspondence from your future husband requesting your hand within the quarter. I daresay you will win yourself a good man. At least one more suited to your . . . requirements than Mr. Clinton."

Amelia tried to settle the dread that roiled in her stomach. She could see no way to squirm her way out of this plight. Yes, she wanted to travel to Brighton, but she had imagined her days there filled with exploration of the seaside and relaxation—not a desperate and pathetic search for a husband. She pushed her hair from her eyes, wishing she had styled the knot tighter.

She could feel her chance of traveling to Brighton slipping away with each second she refused to answer. The words leapt from her throat. "Very well. It seems we have made ourselves a bargain, Papa." She extended her right hand to him.

He looked down at it, a look of amusement flickering over his stern facade.

"Is this not what men do upon striking a bargain?" Amelia gestured at her hand. Her father chuckled—an actual chuckle, one that he didn't mask with a feigned cough. He was far too pleased with this arrangement for her liking.

He shook her hand. The moment he let go, she felt the blood rush from her face. What had she done? She had just guaranteed her own marriage, one way or another. She had just given up all possibility of spinsterhood. Her heart thudded. She could *not* marry Mr. Clinton. It simply wasn't an option. So she would have to meet the perfect man in Brighton and somehow win his heart and an offer of marriage. But she had promised herself years ago that she would never marry. She would not look at her husband the way her mother had looked at her father.

She would not whisper to her children late at night all the things she despised about him.

Her father released her hand. "I'll let you be the one to inform Margaret of your pending adventures. I'll order a carriage. The two of you shall be on your way by Thursday next."

He didn't wait for Amelia to respond. She watched his back as he stepped through the door, closing it behind him.

Her shoulders slumped and she fell back onto her bed, trying to steady her breathing. All in a moment the idea of Brighton had nearly lost its shine. How could she relax and enjoy the excitement of the town if she was expected to flirt with every man that crossed her way? Flirting had never been her strength. And what if she failed to find a suitable man? Not only did she have to find a man better than Mr. Clinton, but she needed to fall in love with him. Love was something people often spent a lifetime in search of, and many, like Margaret and her parents, never did find it. How could Amelia possibly find love in three short months? Such a feat seemed impossible.

She was certain love was only a myth, just like the Brighton waters.

With a deep breath of fortitude, she sat up again. Despite her worries, she couldn't help but smile at the thought of Aunt Margaret's reaction when she received the news of their trip. She would be in absolute raptures; Amelia was certain of it.

Chapter 2

Pacing the damp shoreline for the last hour had done little to calm the rather taut nerves of Adam Claridge. He paused, glancing up at the open sky, a whispered prayer on his lips. *Where was she?* He sat down in the sand, ignoring the cold ocean water seeping through his breeches.

His sister had been missing for almost a fortnight and he hadn't a single idea as to her whereabouts. His days had been spent in continuous and unsuccessful search for her since the day she disappeared. Yet he had achieved nothing. Gathering a fistful of sand, he threw it into the nearby water, cursing under his breath.

"Go home, Adam."

He glanced over his shoulder at the sound of his father's voice. Shaking his head, he returned his gaze to the ocean. The soft crunch of sand underfoot told him that his feeble father was approaching from behind. His father's wrinkled hand settled on his shoulder. "You must rest."

Adam's throat tightened. He couldn't rest. Anxious energy coiled and sprung inside him, searching for answers relentlessly, yet coming up with nothing. He knew he should be tired, for he hadn't slept in forty-eight hours. But his eyes felt as if they were stitched open for fear of missing a clue that might lead him to his sister. Adam turned, crossing his arms, staring at his father's slight frame.

The man was as near death as one could be and remain standing. He had been ill for months. His grey hair rose and fell with the breeze, undulating like the grasses beyond the sand where they stood. His skin hung like loose fabric, marked with creases of laughter and the now-constant creases of worry and fear. Adam couldn't let his father's remaining days be filled with uncertainty and despair. One couldn't have a peaceful death when his daughter was nowhere to be found.

"Go inside, Father. I'm going to find Eleanor." Adam rubbed his eyes against the sting of the salty spray of the ocean. Or was it simply fatigue? The water and sky beyond him blurred into one mass of blue and white.

"How do you expect to find Eleanor by walking the same ten steps repeatedly?" his father questioned. "You may accomplish the same thing by sitting on the sofa within doors. Come now." Mr. Claridge extended his thin arm, the shaking in his muscles evident.

Rather than argue with his father, Adam took one more glance at the ocean before walking up the bank, supporting his father with his arm.

Brighton had been the home of their family for generations, though recently it had become something of a novelty to travelers. The town was deemed a seaside resort, frequented by the Prince Regent since the building of his royal pavilion.

13

Adam had always resented the prince for ordering the construction of the grand building twenty-seven years before. He had been an infant when construction began, and so he had only heard stories of the marvelous view of the sun rising and setting over the ocean that had once been seen from the front window of their home. Instead they now had a clear view of the *marvelous pavilion* that drew so many interested parties to their once quiet town. And now, even more frustrating, he couldn't keep his eyes on the ocean from the comfort of home because his view was so rudely obstructed.

Something drew him to the sea in his search for Eleanor.

"Now, lay down on the sofa and rest." Adam's father hobbled through the doorway behind him, pointing a finger at the powder blue sofa near the window.

Adam rubbed the back of his neck, just now noticing the ache radiating from the top of his spine to the bottom. He laughed, a choked sound.

His father's eyes widened in shock before turning to a gentle rebuke. In two days it seemed Adam had forgotten the correct way to laugh.

"I find it amusing that you are ordering *me* to rest," Adam said, leading his father by the arm toward the sofa. He resisted, clicking his tongue. Lud, the man was stronger than Adam gave him credit.

"If you wish for me to rest then you must rest first. I will not rest until I'm sure that you are not going to do something daft," his father said, his voice scolding.

Adam knew that voice. It meant there was nothing that could be said to change his father's mind. Stubborn was a gentle word for his father's personality. Adam drew a long breath, sitting down on the sofa, keeping his gaze locked with his father's sharp blue eyes. He gave Adam an expectant look, nodding toward his feet, motioning for him to relax.

Adam sighed, lifting his feet onto the sofa and laying his head back. He was too tall for the furniture. His feet hung off the edge of the opposite side. Propping his hand behind his head, he raised his eyebrows for approval until his father nodded in satisfaction.

It was vastly uncomfortable. Since his sixteenth birthday Adam had been too large for this sofa. His father had once had a sturdy frame like his and the same dark hair. Now all they shared in common was the blue eyes and the broken smiles. Adam watched as his father retreated into the hallway, noticing the slumping of his shoulders now that he believed himself to be out of Adam's sight.

It was not fair that his father would have to suffer through so much uncertainty and pain in his final days. He had suffered enough pain already with his illness—he did not deserve to suffer anything else. Adam groaned and tried to sit up, keeping as silent as possible. He could not allow his father to die like this. Adam had to find Eleanor.

He stood from the sofa, ignoring the lightness in his head, and walked carefully across the room to the hall. He passed his father's bedchamber in silence before turning into the study. He lowered himself into a broad leather chair, slapping the side of his face as his eyes drifted closed at the intoxicating smell of fresh parchment. He picked up a quill and readied his parchment. He needed to write down everything he knew before sleep stole his thoughts from him.

The day of Eleanor's disappearance:

Eleanor ate breakfast
Took a morning walk

Returned and took her embroidery outside near one O'clock

Returned for dinner

Left to take an evening walk with Miss Darby, but never arrived at their meeting place.

Gone.

Adam set down the quill, studying the words. It had been an ordinary day. It had taken him a great deal of thought to recall even the information that he *did* remember about Eleanor's whereabouts on the day of her disappearance, little as it was. What could he be missing? Adam had already spoken with Miss Darby and Miss Reed, Eleanor's closest friends, in an attempt to discover any other acquaintances she might have had, any men that might have reason to abduct her. Adam's fists clenched. When he found the one who took her . . .

Visions of broken noses and missing teeth flashed through Adam's mind. The man would wish he had never been born. He prayed she was alive. Eleanor had always been resilient and very firm in her resolutions. She was strong. She had to be alive somewhere, waiting to be found. He would never stop searching. The thought exhausted him and filled him with resolve at once.

His father would see his daughter again; Adam would see to it. He would let nothing stop him, nothing slow his progress, not even sleep. He pushed away from the desk, ready to sneak from the house and show Eleanor's miniature portrait around town again. As he came to his feet, his legs nearly crumpled beneath him and blood rushed from his head. Before he could reach the door his vision flashed in black. He steadied himself, crashing against the doorframe.

"Adam," his father's rasped voice drifted through the hall. More quickly than Adam thought possible, his father stood in front of him, a scowl gathering the loose skin at his brow. A firm index finger extended down the hall to Adam's chamber. "Sleep."

It was as if his father had some power of his renewed determination not to sleep, for all resolve fled and he followed his father's finger toward his chamber. Adam grumbled to himself, feeling very much like a child as his father pulled the blankets up over him.

But before Adam could protest again, his eyes drifted closed, his muscles relaxed, and he fell into a deep and reluctant slumber.

Chapter 3

*A*unt Margaret had never been one to contain her excitement. Or a single other emotion that passed through her large frame.

She had been sitting in an armchair in the library when Amelia had delivered the news that they would soon be traveling to Brighton. Just seconds later, she was on the opposite side of the room, bouncing as if attempting to jump up and down, a motion which her leg would not allow. Amelia stifled her laughter, induced by the raw joy on her aunt's face.

"Thursday next?" her aunt squealed.

"Indeed."

Aunt Margaret covered her mouth, tears filling her turquoise eyes. "Now I may finally take the cure. My leg may be healed, Amelia."

A pang of guilt stabbed at Amelia's chest. It was her

fault Aunt Margaret had become obsessed with the idea of a cure. How could she let her aunt continue with this unrealistic dream? The waters were the same as any other. It was true that seaside air had been known to lift spirits and heal minor ailments, but it couldn't heal Aunt Margaret's physical ailment. Amelia couldn't bring herself to deliver the news to her aunt that she would likely suffer from the pain in her limbs for the rest of her life. There hadn't been a physician capable of helping her, and now she was certain that Brighton could. Tears of joy streamed down her aunt's round, rosy cheeks.

"I am so very excited." She gave a loud sniff. "When do we depart?"

Amelia walked forward and took her hand, her aunt's excitement becoming infectious. "Thursday next."

"Thursday next!"

Amelia nodded, grinning once again.

Aunt Margaret pushed back her blonde curls, blinking in rapid thought. "We must purchase bathing clothes, when we arrive, for we mustn't be seen dipping nude." Her eyes widened. "I do hope our dipper is a robust woman, for I should hate to die of a drowning."

Amelia found herself fighting laughter once again. Though her trip had been ruined by the requirements her father had set upon her, at least she would get to experience the many adventures that would come from having her aunt as a traveling companion. But if her aunt thought Amelia planned to dip as well, she was mistaken. Amelia had no interest in wading into the ocean to be lowered into the water by a strange woman—an employed 'dipper' of the seaside town.

Amelia dreamt of swimming out in the shallows on her own, feeling the cool, wet sand sinking between her toes and the salty breeze kissing her cheeks, an abundance of sunshine whisking the moisture away from her skin. But the image was quickly blotted out by images of ballrooms and card tables surrounded by young gentlemen. Amelia would have little time for solitary adventures if she were to find herself a suitable husband.

Her heart sunk but she ignored it.

"It is likely that Brighton sells very suitable bathing clothes. We shall pick some up for you in town. My father is going to rent a lovely little house for us. I do hope we find enough entertainment to occupy our time. We will be staying for a quarter year, after all."

"A quarter year! That should allow ample time for the cure to take effect. I shall bathe daily in the waters."

Amelia chewed her lip against the barbed truth. Oh, how it would sting when her aunt's hopes came crashing to the ground. She decided a change of subject was in order.

"There *is* one stipulation tied to this excursion, and I will need your help. My papa has allowed us to travel to Brighton . . . but only if I return engaged. Therefore, it seems my days will be filled with more flirtations and sociality than I would like." Amelia sighed. "I had hoped to read mysterious novels by the seaside while you take your . . . dips."

Aunt Margaret's eyes widened in shock. "You are to return engaged? How ever will you accomplish that?"

Amelia willed herself not to be offended by her aunt's implications. "I will need your help."

Her aunt burst into a bout of hearty laughter, bending over at the waist. "I daresay I am not the primary consultant you should be seeking. I know nothing of the art of catching a husband."

"Oh, perhaps you will be surprised at your hidden abilities. Perhaps you have had them all along, but you simply lacked the courage to use those abilities." Amelia began pacing the room, wringing her hands together. "My stomach has itself in knots at the prospect of finding a husband." Even as she said the words her stomach seemed to fold in half. How selective could she be with the little time she had? Would the man she married be just like Mr. Clinton after all?

"Hush, child. Do not worry yourself over it. Surely my brother will understand should you return unattached."

Amelia shook her head numbly. "He will not. It was agreed that I would marry Mr. Clinton should I fail in Brighton."

Aunt Margaret grimaced. "Mr. Clinton? The man with the cane and the greying hair?"

"I'm afraid so." Amelia said through a sigh.

Her aunt had begun fanning her face, the flush returning to her cheeks. "Oh, dear. Even I would not come within my cane's length of that man." She gripped Amelia's arm. "Not to worry. We will find you a husband in little time at all. Think nothing of it your first month in Brighton—let it be everything you dreamed of. After that we will begin our search in earnest."

Amelia's palms began to sweat. It was easier said than done, to be sure. *Drat.* She truly had landed herself in a quandary. How could she enjoy any time in Brighton knowing she would soon have to engage in a wild husband hunt?

"Let us reverse it," Amelia said. "I will find a man to marry within our first month in Brighton. Then we may enjoy the rest of the trip."

"With a man to entertain," her aunt said.

"Hopefully a man I love, so I will not mind at all." Even as Amelia said the words she didn't believe them. Love was an unrealistic dream.

Aunt Margaret picked up her cane from where it rested against the wall. Moving to a desk near a tall bookshelf, she readied a piece of parchment.

"What are you doing?" Amelia approached her, taking a seat in the leather armchair across from her aunt.

Aunt Margaret froze as she dipped the quill in the inkwell. "I am writing a list. If I am to help you, I will need to know the qualities you are searching for in this man." She positioned the quill at the top of the paper, awaiting Amelia's response.

"Oh, er—well, he must not be ridiculous."

Not ridiculous, Aunt Margaret wrote.

"He must be charming, kind, and patient."

Margaret's hand hurried across the page, her arm shaking with the effort.

"Handsome," Amelia shrugged. "And much younger than Mr. Clinton, but well-bred and mature," she added.

Aunt Margaret's quill moved faster.

"Honest, intelligent, gentle, and entertaining. And positively . . . lovely. In the most masculine way, of course."

"Good heavens, child. How ever do you expect to find a man such as this? I wouldn't think it possible." Aunt Margaret stretched her fingers.

Perhaps that was why Aunt Margaret never married in her youth. Her expectations had been high as well, and she had given up on the existence of such a gentleman. Amelia pushed away her doubts. He had to exist. *He had to.*

"We are simply adding a bit more mystery and intrigue to our adventure," Amelia said. "If fate brings this man to Brighton, we are charged with the task of finding him and forcing him into a happy marriage with me." Amelia chewed her lip. That sounded absolutely horrible. Why should such a wonderful man even be interested in marrying her?

Aunt Margaret seemed to puzzle on this before scratching out her list and replacing it with two words. *Lord Lovely.* "We shall call him 'Lord Lovely.' Until you meet him and discover his true name, of course."

Amelia couldn't help but laugh. 'Lord Lovely' sounded positively agreeable, especially when spoken by Aunt Margaret with her thoughtful, serious expression. "Very well. I shall find this Lord Lovely, sweep him out of his boots, and marry him. How difficult shall it be?"

Aunt Margaret's smile fell in an instant. "Very difficult," she mused.

Oh. Amelia had been expecting encouragement. She found herself chewing the nail of her thumb. She couldn't allow herself to worry over it too much. Falling in love was a natural thing, at least from the stories and books she had entertained herself with. But unlike those books, her own finding love came with a designated time limit.

Amelia clapped her hands together in finality. "Let us begin packing our trunks. It will not be a quick task. Perhaps I might convince my father to allow me to have a new gown made. Or two. He cannot expect me to catch a husband with my old ones. That certainly should have been part of our accord. I will go speak with him right now." Amelia turned toward the door.

"See to it that you widdle a new gown for myself into your arrangement." Aunt Margaret threw her a wink.

Amelia smiled. "Of course. My escort *must* be dressed to the height of fashion as well."

Her aunt gave a hearty chuckle, causing her cheeks to shake and a second chin to appear beneath her first. Amelia had never met a more endearing woman. She loved her aunt immensely. She wanted to believe—to have hope that the cure of the Brighton waters held some merit. How sad it would be if her aunt's health declined further in the coming years.

Amelia left the library refreshed and determined. There was no sense in skirting around her new duty with timidity. She was going to Brighton, where social rules were often thrown to the sea, where the gentlemen were plenty, the skies were bright, and where the waters held a magical cure. From the sound of that, adventure certainly awaited her.

Chapter 4

$\mathcal{A}$melia had never known her father to be so generous. So pleased was he with the prospect of her pending marriage, that he allowed her *three* new gowns as well as one for Aunt Margaret. He didn't even put a limit on the allowed embellishments. Lace, ribbons, layers and layers of taffeta. The trip to the mantua maker had certainly brightened Amelia's spirits.

The following week was filled with preparations, and to Amelia's surprise, a lack of worry within her. There was something about the companionship of her aunt and new gowns that brought her confidence. Her father had even agreed to send her with a maid that could assist with the hairstyling and dressing of the pair. Amelia was relieved to find that her mornings would not be spent assisting Aunt Margaret into her corset.

The day of their departure Amelia embraced her father,

trying to ignore the feelings of betrayal that clenched in her chest. She reminded herself that she had put herself in this situation—her father wasn't entirely to blame for it.

"Farewell, Papa," she said in a tight voice.

"Farewell." He gave her arm a squeeze and his lips almost curved into a cherishing smile. Almost. "I suspect you will find a very eligible man, Amelia."

She swallowed and gave him a firm nod. It was all she could manage. Words were difficult when encased with a slew of emotions.

Climbing into the carriage, she dropped down on the cushions beside the maid that would be accompanying them. Fanny was her name, and she was close to Amelia's age. She had rather short, dark hair, and a bright, inviting countenance. The journey would take all of two days, so Amelia had brought with her a small bag filled with things to occupy her time. Knitting, embroidery, three different novels, one of which she had found discarded on the street near the mantua maker's shop. It appeared to be a book of mysteries and riddles of sorts.

"Godspeed!" Aunt Margaret exclaimed as she ducked into the carriage. Amelia clutched her seat as it rocked beneath her aunt's weight. Her father's face reddened with exertion as he pushed Aunt Margaret into the carriage from behind. She dropped her cane down beside Amelia, grinning.

Aunt Margaret's face fell as she studied Amelia's sullen expression. "Are you not thrilled?"

"I am." Amelia eyed her father as he closed the door behind them. She leaned toward her aunt. "I am only nervous. That is all. You know why."

Her aunt pursed her lips. "I'm afraid I do not know why."

"The husband hunt," Amelia reminded her.

"Oh, yes." Her aunt gave her a look of heartfelt understanding. "But that is a minimal dilemma. We will have it solved and over with in a single month, and then we may enjoy the remainder of the summer in peace and serenity." She touched the tips of her index fingers to her thumbs and raised her arms, closing her eyes. They shot open, a flash of piercing blue. "We must review our list during our journey!" She reached down the neckline of her peach gown, withdrawing a crumpled sheet of parchment from beneath a bustle of pleated peach trim.

Amelia shook her head. "I do not wish to make this journey any more uncomfortable than it is already bound to be." It seemed Amelia's legs were already tightening and aching as the coachman set the horses in motion. It would be a long journey. She waved out the window at her father.

Aunt Margaret watched the exchange, and when Amelia faced her again she caught her aunt's grimace. "That man must realize he isn't serving your happiness by forcing a marriage upon you. Perhaps he might untwist his breeches and rub the dirt from his eyes in order to finally think and see clearly." She huffed a breath before crossing her arms.

Fanny covered her mouth to hide her smile. She certainly couldn't be seen laughing at her master's expense. Amelia chuckled. She often didn't understand the words her aunt said, but she vastly enjoyed them anyway.

"I have a book for us to study during our travels." Amelia dug through her bag and withdrew the book that contained the riddles. The pages were stained in dirt and wrinkled from past water damage. "It will challenge our minds, and I expect it will give your memory a beneficial amount of exercise."

Her aunt clapped her hands together. "How perfect."

Amelia peeled the pages open—they stuck slightly together. She hoped this book would pass the time and help distract her from her fears. The next two days of travel would be long, and she needed every distraction she could get. For when she arrived in Brighton there would be no time for distraction, only for duty. She took a deep breath. "Page one."

The two days that followed were filled with smelly inns and cramped legs, vomiting (from carriage sickness and unappetizing meals), and many complicated riddles found within the book Amelia had opened. She found she wanted to do little else other than work through the riddles in her mind. The book was fascinating, and she found that she possessed quite the talent for solving these abstract problems. One riddle involving a fish and a bird, she solved within five minutes, while her aunt had struggled through it for all of three hours.

By dusk on the second day, the coachman announced that they were only three miles from their destination. He had warned them of highwaymen on the roads between London and Brighton, but they had yet to encounter any threatening men in venetian masks. Amelia breathed a sigh of relief. She did not fare well with danger.

Amelia could smell the ocean. Perhaps it was only her imagination, but when she closed her eyes, the aroma of salty, crisp water and clean, bright air filled her nose and lungs. How different it would be from the cramped and overcrowded air that permeated the streets of Nottingham. There would be room to move, to breathe, to discover the potential that had been stirring within the confines of her hometown and caged heart. Perhaps it would be beneficial to search for the possibility of love among such free circumstances.

"Look!" Aunt Margaret pointed out the window. Amelia's heart lurched. Were highwaymen descending upon them? She scrambled closer to the window and relief flooded through her. Her aunt's bejeweled finger extended in the direction of the ocean. Amelia gasped. If only it weren't so dim outside. She strained her eyes to see her surroundings, excitement coursing through her limbs. But the darkness hid most of what she so longed to see. She reminded herself that there would be much to explore in the morning.

Under the dim light of the moon, the ocean shifted in the distance, a dark and beautiful thing, moving about as the wind threw shafts of water into the air and transformed them into waves. The sky met the sea in a line of peach—the place where the sun had just recently fell and disappeared. Small buildings and houses curved around the beach in tightly knit lines, and in the distance, a large building stood out from the rest. Amelia knew it was the royal pavilion, built for the Prince Regent himself.

"How beautiful," Amelia breathed into the glass of the window. The seaside town appeared larger than she had imagined it before. There would be many wonders to discover—and many gentlemen to meet.

Her father had rented them a small home near the town center in which they would be living for the summer. Ten minutes later, the coachman parked in front of the little house, helping Aunt Margaret down from the carriage first. She stumbled to her feet, her eyes watching everything but the ground as she descended from the step.

"We are here! We are in Brighton!" Aunt Margaret kissed her own hand and patted the coachman's face. He stepped back, lowering his gaze to hide the shock in his expression. Amelia's eyes widened before she erupted in laughter. A footman from within their home met them at the carriage, assisting Amelia in her descent first. Climbing down from the step, she stretched her legs and back, inhaling deeply the seaside air. Their maid, Fanny stepped down behind her, fascination burning in her eyes as she looking in the direction of the sea.

After the footman brought in their belongings, the butler welcomed them and closed the door of the house. It was a small space, but would be sufficient for their needs. Fanny retrieved a set of matches from her trunk before setting to work lighting more candles, bringing the interiors of the house into sharp focus.

"I hope you will find this home suitable for your visit," said the butler, who had introduced himself as Mr. Reeves. "The home is equipped with two footmen, a cook, and myself."

Amelia yawned, thanking Mr. Reeves with a delayed smile.

"'Tis time for you to sleep, miss," Fanny said. "I'll be arranging your hair quite special in the morning." She winked at her. Although Fanny hadn't asked questions, Amelia suspected she knew of the lofty task she was here to accomplish, and therefore knew Amelia would require an extraordinary hair arrangement to do it.

"Thank you, Fanny." Amelia yawned again. "The bedrooms are down the hall, I presume." She hadn't realized how tired she was until that yawn had escaped her. Now her feet seemed to weigh tons and her eyelashes as well.

"I must ensure your rooms are prepared." Fanny hurried ahead of her and pushed open the nearest door in the hallway. Amelia smiled through half-lidded eyes as she passed through the doorway. The bed, clothed in white sheets and a thick quilt, appeared to Amelia to be a sanctuary of the most heavenly kind.

"What activities shall we pursue tomorrow?" Aunt Margaret entered the room, her face glowing with excitement. Amelia wondered how the woman managed to have so much energy despite her ailments. Even now, as Aunt Margaret leaned heavily on her cane, she continued to sport an exuberant smile.

Amelia fell back on her bed, rubbing her hands down the soft quilt. "First we must venture to the ocean. I cannot wait to see the grandeur of it under a morning sun." She sighed. It would be a perfect, peaceful start to their trip.

"Oh, yes. That is a splendid idea. Then afterward we might venture to a nearby assembly room for some socialization." Her aunt winked.

Amelia already dreaded it. She released a long groan as she closed her eyes, covering her face with her hand. "Perhaps I might stay here in Brighton forever and never face Papa again. If I do not return, he cannot force me to marry."

She heard the blunt sound of Aunt Margaret's cane hitting the ground, followed by soft steps coming closer to her. Aunt Margaret peeled Amelia's hand off her face, staring down at her with reprimand. "You will succeed."

"But I have always wished to be a spinster like you, Aunt Margaret. The notion is so rebellious and defiant and . . . brilliantly empowering."

A little smile broke through Aunt Margaret's scowl. "I'm afraid the time has passed for such aspirations. You made a bargain, and you must keep your word."

"We will ensure you are looking beautiful tomorrow, miss." Fanny nodded from across the room as she finished unpacking Amelia's belongings. "Both of you."

Aunt Margaret stepped back from Amelia's bed and smoothed the wisps of blonde hair that had escaped her spinster knot. She smiled demurely. "Oh, yes. There are new waters ahead, my dear. I do believe that is both a literal and a figurative statement." Then she left the room, chuckling as she went.

Chapter 5

The waters were every bit as frustrating to Adam as they had been a week before. The sky had only begun to split with white light—the first hint of morning. Adam had slept all afternoon the day he had last ventured to the coast, only to awaken to moonlight streaming through his windows. He had evaluated his notes all night, trying to recall the details he had missed that might help him find Eleanor. He had spent the week speaking to people in town, searching for any knowledge those strangers might have had. He had found little success.

With a sigh of frustration, Adam bent down and tossed a large stone into the calm ocean. The resulting splash was less than satisfying. Searching the sand, he found a larger stone, casting it into the water again. The motion became a welcome distraction, so he took to gathering a large pile of stones before thrusting them all into the water with renewed vigor. His right arm ached with the effort after what must have been the twentieth stone. He fought back the emotion rising inside him, but it came out in a well-timed grunt instead, splitting the air as he flung another piece of heavy rock at the ocean.

Just as the rock sunk beneath the surface, he heard something—a sort of feminine giggling. His heart dropped. The laugh sounded almost exactly like Eleanor's. He whirled around to face the sound, his legs stiff and eyes wild. If she dared to come back here after he had been worried for days, only to *laugh* at him, he would have her head.

His face froze as he took in the image before him. The party of two ladies that stood in open entertainment of his stone casting display did not contain Eleanor. He grumbled under his breath as the younger of the two ladies covered her mouth to hide her laughter. The other lady, a large woman with a cane, clambered toward him with alarming speed.

"And what do you think you are doing to the precious waters of Brighton, sir?" The woman's voice grew louder as she approached him. "I cannot be taking my dip with such large stones floating about my feet."

"Aunt Margaret ..." The younger woman picked up her skirts, following her supposed aunt in an apparent attempt to calm her. Adam noticed the woman's feet were bare as she stepped through the damp sand. Catching his gaze, she dropped her skirts, clearly flustered.

She cleared her throat, focusing her attention on her companion. "Aunt Margaret, I do not believe stones *float*." She eyed Adam carefully. "If they did, this man's recent— er—activity would have been vastly counterproductive."

He couldn't help but stare at her as she came closer, momentarily taken by surprise at the beauty of her features. The dark blonde of her hair fell attractively around her face, and her eyes, a deep brown, sparked with knowledge and life.

The young woman took hold of her aunt's arm. "Let us find a separate embankment to explore," she whispered, as if he couldn't hear her.

Adam mustered up a smile. "No, I insist. Stay. I will take my leave." He ran his hand over his disheveled hair, cringing at the thought of how he must have appeared, throwing stones into the water in a fit of anger. The young woman studied him, one brow raised in speculation. Her brown eyes sparked with curiosity, and he paused to notice once again how pretty they were.

"But it is clear you were not yet finished," she said, motioning at the pile of rocks at his feet. "Do not allow us to disturb you."

Adam barely caught the shakiness in her voice, the laughter she seemed to be hiding. His stone-throwing had not frightened her, at least. But something about her laughter at his expense plucked a string of annoyance within him. These women did not understand the seriousness of the situation. Eleanor was missing. He stepped around the rocks and came closer. "May I inquire after your name?"

She hesitated, exchanging a look with her companion before saying, "I am Miss Amelia Buxton, and this is my aunt, Miss Margaret Buxton."

"A pleasure, Miss Amelia, Miss Buxton." He gave them a curt nod. "I know you find my frustrations quite fascinating to observe, but I will leave you to it if you don't mind." Adam gave the ladies a nod and turned to move his agonized pacing to a different area of the beach.

"I do indeed mind." Miss Amelia's soft voice stopped

him. "I'm afraid you have left us with two pestering items of curiosity. You simply cannot desert us now."

Her aunt nodded, catching her balance on her cane.

Adam was losing patience now. All he wanted to do was find his sister. He reminded himself that it was possible that these ladies could have seen her. Perhaps they had information that could lead to her safe return home. There were hundreds of new visitors brought to Brighton every week, but it was worth inquiring.

"And what items would those be?" he asked.

Miss Amelia tapped her chin. "I am curious because you never told me your name, or what it is that has you so frustrated."

He sighed. "My name is Adam Claridge."

She nodded. "And your frustration?"

Adam schooled himself to be polite. Who was this woman to meddle in business that wasn't her own? "My sister has been missing for a fortnight now. I have little idea where to find her, or what may have happened to her."

"Oh, dear." This came from the aunt, her full cheeks falling in sorrow.

"How dreadful," Miss Amelia said. "Perhaps we might help you find her." Her face showed true sincerity, and while Adam found it endearing, he knew there was likely nothing she could do to help him.

Deciding it could not hinder his efforts to try, he said, "Perhaps you have seen her. She is near your height. She has dark hair, nearly black. Her eyes are blue and look very much like mine." Adam leaned forward, allowing the ladies a long look at his eyes. He wanted to ensure the image was ingrained in each of them, perchance they met Eleanor on the street she would appear familiar. Miss Amelia squinted at his eyes, as if memorizing every detail.

He took the opportunity to study her eyes as well, the dark sweep of lashes and rich brown. After several seconds, she gave a firm nod.

"Have you seen her?" he asked.

"I have not. I'm afraid we have only just arrived here yesterday. But we will certainly keep our eyes open, won't we, Aunt Margaret?"

Any hope Adam had dared to feel dropped within him, filling his stomach with dread once again. These women would be of no help in finding his sister. He watched his boot as it kicked the sand.

"You might help us find someone as well," the older woman said.

He glanced up wearily. "You are in search of someone?"

"Yes, as a matter of fact, we are looking to find Miss Amelia a husb—"

Before she could finish, Miss Amelia threw herself between Adam and her aunt, going so far as to cover her aunt's lips with her palm, ending her words in a firm slapping sound. Adam's eyes widened.

Miss Amelia gave an awkward laugh, dropping her hand. Adam heard her whisper something to her aunt before turning back toward him. The color in her cheeks deepened to a rosy pink as she smiled.

"My apologies, Mr. Claridge."

He fought the grin of disbelief and amusement that tugged at his lips. It was a welcome distraction, for he hadn't felt the urge to smile in days. The elder Miss Buxton rubbed her wrist against her mouth with a huffed breath. "Your hand tastes of sand, Amelia."

Miss Amelia brushed her hands against her skirts, avoiding Adam's gaze. He chuckled under his breath. Of course she was here in search of a husband. She had not stopped her aunt's words quickly enough to keep them from his notice. There were hundreds of young women that travelled to Brighton to experience the variety of social activities and to pick through the crowd of eligible gentlemen that came to do the same. Eleanor had often complained of the ladies that came from out of town, that they decreased her chances of ever finding a match in Brighton. Adam, though he fancied one day marrying, had been occupied in caring for his father and sister for too long to make an effort at courting. And now, with Eleanor lost, he could think of nothing else but bringing her home to safety.

Miss Amelia didn't seem inclined to surrender. "Perhaps I might help you find your sister with the information you already have of the day she disappeared."

Adam eyed her carefully before shaking his head. "I have already sorted through it hundreds of times in my mind."

"Yes, but you possess the mind of a man. Myself, and your sister, have minds of a . . . different sort. That very well may be what you are missing in your investigation, Mr. Claridge." She smiled, stepping forward with a curtsy. "A woman."

"A woman?"

"Please, don't look so appalled! We are quite intelligent, you know." She tapped the side of her head to indicate the *intelligence* she boasted of.

Adam wondered if it was worth giving this woman the satisfaction of helping him.

"We are quite intelligent, indeed." The elder Miss Buxton lifted her cane to tap the side of her head with it. She seemed to misjudge the distance, knocking the side of her skull with great force. She staggered to the side, nearly toppling over. She clutched her niece for balance.

Adam held back his laughter, pressing his lips together to contain it.

"You are not supporting my argument of our intelligence, Aunt Margaret," Miss Amelia said through her laughter. Adam paused to listen to the hearty, joyful sound. She had a pleasant laugh, one that reminded him of Eleanor.

The elder Miss Buxton snorted, erupting in laughter of her own, rubbing the side of her head gingerly. "I am intelligent the majority of the time. But for the moments that I am not so intelligent," she motioned at the ocean ahead, "I seek the Brighton waters to cure me. I take my first dip at first light on the morrow."

Adam scoffed much more loudly than he intended. The cure of the Brighton waters? It was sought after by only the most desperate of people…and the most credulous. He cleared his throat when he noticed the glaring that both women had directed at him. "My apologies, but I fear the notion that the Brighton waters contain a cure is entirely false. It is only a way to lure tourists to the resort, nothing more."

The older woman planted one hand on her hip. "You are wrong. The waters will cure my leg and they will cure my ailing memory as well. Amelia believes such things as well."

Adam's gaze shifted to her, studying her somewhat guilty expression. She caught his eye and cleared her expression with a nod. "Yes, it is worth a try, to be sure."

Adam narrowed his eyes in doubt of her words. She was far too intelligent to believe such nonsense. He stopped himself. Intelligent? Had he not just ruled out such a possibility?

"Ah. It seems my hope of your intelligence was in vain if you believe in such a cure," he said. "You cannot help me find my sister. Good day." He gave the ladies a nod and turned on his heel. He estimated that it would take no more than three paces before Miss Amelia would stop him in order to defend her intellect.

"Excuse me, Mr. Claridge, but I find that to be rather presumptuous."

Adam stopped in the process of his third step, masking his smile before facing the ladies once again. "How so? Have you any proof that the Brighton waters contain a 'magical remedy?'"

She pursed her lips. "I believe intelligence requires an open mind—a mind that sees the irrational thought to carry as much possibility as the rational."

"Are you admitting that the cure of the Brighton waters is an irrational idea?"

She exchanged a look with her aunt. "Yes, irrational, but not impossible."

Adam stopped himself from rolling his eyes, for he didn't want Miss Amelia to have any further reason to dislike him. Despite his misgivings, he wondered if she truly did have the ability to help him find Eleanor. There was something about her that he was drawn to, a certain hope that she instilled in his heart.

Adam released a puff of breath, changing the subject. "If you believe you can help me, you must know the events of the day Eleanor disappeared. First, she took a morning walk on our property. She then returned to our home, taking her embroidery outside. She returned for dinner, and then took an evening walk with a woman by the name of Miss Darby, of whom I have spoken with previously. Miss Darby said that Eleanor never arrived at their meeting place."

Miss Amelia listened intently, her smooth brow furrowing in concentration. "Is this all the information you possess?"

"Unfortunately, yes." Adam said.

For several seconds she stood in silence. "Who is this Miss Darby to Eleanor?"

"A dear friend."

"I see. When you spoke to her regarding Eleanor's disappearance, how was she faring?"

Adam tried to recall the exchange in his mind. Miss Darby had been in her drawing room when he called upon her, stitching upon a bonnet. He could envision the crimson of the draperies and the bright sunlight reflecting off Miss Darby's youthful face. Her expression . . . it had appeared rather alarmed at his arrival at her home. Yes, she had acted strangely when questioned, but in Adam's opinion, Miss Darby had always been an odd young lady.

"She was faring quite well," he said in a foggy voice, recalling the absent look on Miss Darby's face. Considering that her dearest friend was missing, she was indeed faring *quite well.*

Miss Amelia's soft voice recalled his attention. "Did she shed a tear?"

He blinked. "No, not one."

"Did she exhibit any sign of remorse, any at all?"

Adam thought once again of Miss Darby's face, shrouded in sunlit curls, sitting in front of the open draperies. She had answered his questions with politeness, but had not asked any in return. Had she seemed slightly nervous at his presence in her home? He remembered her small hands wringing together as she spoke. In fact, it did not seem to trouble her at all when he declared that Eleanor had yet to be found.

Miss Amelia gave her aunt a heartfelt look, and both women shook their heads. "If my dearest friend were to disappear against my knowledge, I would not dismiss it without a tear. I doubt any woman would."

One phrase stood out to Adam. "Against your knowledge?"

Miss Amelia took one step closer to him. Her eyes locked on his, the depth of her gaze catching him by surprise. "I cannot be certain, but I believe Miss Darby knows more than she is revealing, Mr. Claridge. I would advise you to speak with her again."

A shiver settled between Adam's shoulder blades, stretching out to his arms and fingertips. It was clear to him now that Miss Darby had not behaved naturally. How had he skipped over such an important detail? He raked his hand over his hair, taking a step back to think. He wanted to run to Miss Darby's house immediately.

"I wish you all good fortune in finding your sister," Miss Amelia said.

Adam returned his gaze to her, his mind racing. "I thank you, and I apologize for any misjudgments I may have cast upon you." He gave her a quick smile and gave each lady a nod before taking stride in the direction he knew Miss Darby to live. He would not be taken as a fool. If she knew anything, he would uncover it.

Chapter 6

"I declare I have never met such a stern man in my life!" Aunt Margaret's eyes rolled back into her head in a dramatic fashion.

Amelia laughed. "His sister is missing. He has every reason to be stern." She looked down at the narrow path they walked upon. The assembly rooms were a short distance from the area of the beach they had found Mr. Claridge, thankfully, for Amelia doubted Aunt Margaret's legs could endure a distance much further.

Aunt Margaret gasped. "Are you defending the man?"

"No, I am simply giving him a fair judgement." Yes, Mr. Claridge had been stern, but how could he not be at such a time? He had also been remarkably handsome. Amelia knew that Aunt Margaret could not have possibly missed that detail. Of course appearances did not excuse poor behavior, but even if Mr. Claridge had resembled the back end of a horse, Amelia would still have felt sympathy toward him. She did not have any siblings of her own, but she knew she would have a fierce protection for them if she did.

Amid her deep thought, Amelia failed to notice her aunt's look of suspicious amusement.

"You fancy him." She pointed a plump finger at Amelia's face in accusation. She gave a deep chuckle. "It is my humble opinion that you should pursue a man of a more joyful, optimistic disposition."

"I do not have a mind to pursue him, Aunt Margaret! Not to worry. But he does need our help." Amelia tried to push the sorrow she had seen in Mr. Claridge's eyes out of her mind, but it lingered there like smoke above a fire. The poor man. She hoped he found the information he was looking for when he spoke to that suspicious Miss Darby.

Aunt Margaret smiled. "That is very well, for there are still hundreds of men to be met here in Brighton. You will please your father yet."

Amelia hardly heard her. It was still so disheartening that this adventure was marred by the expectation of an engagement. If only Amelia could find a way out of her agreement with her father. She bit her lip in guilt.

Aunt Margaret rambled on about her plans for their trip while Amelia tried to keep down her breakfast as she thought of the desired outcome of her trip. Seeing the assembly rooms as they approached, full and alive with many eligible young men, made Amelia's heart catch in her throat.

Aunt Margaret's voice reentered Amelia's ears. "...I have hired two sedan chairs as well as a bathing machine for two persons, scheduled for the early morning tomorrow."

"Two?" Amelia stopped her.

"Yes, the sedan chairs will carry us through the steep path to the dipping area, and we will change into our dipping clothes in the bathing machines. You did not plan on changing freely, did you Amelia?" She cast her a look of disapproval.

"No! Of course not! I did not plan on changing at all."

"You cannot be dipped in your dress."

Amelia puffed out a breath of frustration. Her aunt already knew she did not want to be dipped in the waters. "I did not plan to dip at all."

"Why ever not?" Aunt Margaret gave a frown.

"I haven't any physical ailments in need of curing."

"That you do not." A sultry male voice came from Amelia's side. She jerked her gaze to the right. A man stood there, tall, sturdy, with dark blonde hair that had been roughly combed. He wore an elaborate blue waistcoat, embroidered with silver threads. His cravat was secured loosely, leaving space for his distinct jawline to be seen. His sharp blue and very handsome eyes gazed down at Amelia unabashedly. "Never before have I been witness to such beauty."

She couldn't quite believe what she was hearing. It was irrational, to be sure. "Pardon me?"

The man chuckled, straightening the lapels of his jacket. He leaned his head down closer, capturing her gaze in his. "I would be glad to flatter you further but I'm afraid we have not made our introductions."

Amelia stopped her disgust from showing. This man considered himself to be very charming, arrogantly so, a quality that Amelia didn't find charming at all. As manners were not paramount here in Brighton, she had half a mind to walk away from him without a word.

Aunt Margaret's elbow dug into Amelia's side, causing

her to step quickly away—and closer to the presumptuous man.

Her face burned as she saw the look of satisfaction on his face. "I am Miss Amelia Buxton."

"And I am Miss Amelia's aunt, Miss Margaret Buxton." Aunt Margaret's voice carried a flirtatious note that made Amelia cringe. It seemed that while his attempted charms had not won Amelia's favor, they had taken the desired effect upon her aunt.

"A pleasure to meet you both. I am Edward Beaumont, Lord Ramsbury by courtesy. My father is the earl of Coventry." The man's gaze settled on Amelia. "What brings you to Brighton?"

Amelia could sense Aunt Margaret's approval. This man bore a title, or a courtesy one at least. He would one day be an earl. He seemed quite young, likely no older than twenty-five.

"We are seeking the cure of the Brighton waters," Amelia said before Aunt Margaret could announce that Amelia was searching for a husband. "We dip on the morrow."

Perhaps the man would leave her alone if he thought her to be mad enough to believe the cure. Mr. Claridge had found the cure completely ridiculous, so surely Lord Ramsbury would feel the same.

Lord Ramsbury flashed her a smile. "So I suspected. The cure is without fail. I expect you shall be even closer to perfect on the morrow after your dip, though I doubt such a thing to be possible."

Aunt Margaret grinned as if she had just been flattered herself. She was enjoying Lord Ramsbury's display far more than Amelia. Despite her every effort, Amelia's cheeks ripened with a severe blush. "Oh, I assure you, I am far from perfection."

Lord Ramsbury opened his mouth to speak, so Amelia quickly added, "and I am not inviting you to flatter me further by saying so."

He gave a deep chuckle. "Your humility is very diverting, Miss Amelia."

"That is still flattery."

"Amelia!" Aunt Margaret's elbow found her side once again, and Amelia grunted as the pain shot into her ribs.

Lord Ramsbury's eyes widened, the blueness unlike anything Amelia had seen. He truly was handsome, and titled, and quite interested in her. She stopped herself. A man like Lord Ramsbury was a rake and a scoundrel, and his flattery was not exclusive to Amelia, she knew that for certain.

He cleared his throat, choosing to ignore Aunt Margaret's display. "Is this your first visit to Brighton?"

"Indeed," Amelia said.

"Then allow me to give you a tour of the assembly rooms." He gestured at the doors of the crowded space.

She hesitated, but knew that Aunt Margaret would drag her along if she refused. "Very well."

Lord Ramsbury smiled again, this time with a touch more sincerity. He extended one arm to Amelia and the other to Aunt Margaret. Amelia took his arm, waiting for Aunt Margaret to join her on the other side. She shot her aunt a look of desperation from behind Lord Ramsbury's back.

Aunt Margaret shook her head. "I should like to rest my leg for a spell. I will allow you to take Miss Amelia on this tour alone." Only Amelia could hear the devious edge to her aunt's voice.

Amelia opened her mouth to protest, but stopped. She had not given Lord Ramsbury a chance. Yes, he was a ridiculous flirt, but if she claimed to be in possession of an open mind, she needed to refrain from making any hasty judgements.

"Very well, Miss Buxton, if you are certain. I hope your leg finds recovery." Lord Ramsbury seemed far too pleased with the arrangement.

"Oh, yes, I am certain." Aunt Margaret found a place on a nearby bench between two rose bushes. As Amelia turned away with Lord Ramsbury, she caught Aunt Margaret's wide grin of amusement.

"You will meet many wonderful people here in Brighton," Lord Ramsbury said as they entered the doors of the first floor of the assembly rooms. Even in day the room was full of people, and the evening festivities had yet to begin. Light music floated in the air as people moved about, engaging in new conversations and flirtations. The sight made Amelia's hands slick with sweat. How could she be so social? She had little experience in the matter. Her father's requirement had begun to feel far out of reach, and she had only been in Brighton a day.

"Brighton feels to me like an extension of London," he continued. "I have lived here all my life, and am very well known in the town. I have yet to meet a frequent visitor of Brighton that does not know my name."

Amelia looked up at his pompous smile, and couldn't stop her words. "Do you consider yourself to be one of these 'wonderful people' that I am bound to meet?"

He met her eyes with a smirk. "Of course, there are none here as wonderful as me."

Only when his smile widened did Amelia realize he was jesting—or was he? By the sway in his step she could only conclude that his words held some merit.

"Have I nothing to look forward to then?" she said in

a teasing voice. "If all people that I meet are bound to be beneath you, I ought to lower my expectation significantly."

Lord Ramsbury looked surprised at first, then exploded into laughter. Amelia bit her lip. She was glad her words had not taken true offense.

He stopped walking, taking hold of her arm and turning to look more directly at her. They stood near the north wall of the large space, and Amelia felt vulnerable under the sharp daggers being thrown at her through the gazes of many apparently jealous women throughout the room.

"I declare I have never met a woman like you," Lord Ramsbury said.

Amelia didn't believe him for a moment. "I am honored. Certainly you have met many, *many* women. Perhaps you have even uttered that very phrase to dozens."

His brow furrowed. Oh, no. Amelia had taken her quips too far. Before she could hear his reply, a man stepped up beside him, planting a hand on Lord Ramsbury's shoulder.

"George!" Lord Ramsbury grasped the man's hand behind him. "I didn't know you were stationed at Brighton once again."

Amelia stood nearby, watching the exchange. The man, George, wore the bright red coat of the regiment. As Amelia surveyed the room, she saw several men dressed similarly. With the prince in frequent residence of Brighton, measures were often taken to ensure his safety.

Lord Ramsbury motioned Amelia forward. "Allow me to introduce to you, Miss Amelia Buxton."

The man gave a brief nod. "Mr. George Vane. A pleasure."

Amelia nodded in return. Recognizing an opportunity to escape the less than pleasant company of Lord Ramsbury, she turned to him. "I need to go outside and ensure my aunt is well."

He hesitated. "Of course. Will you return? I haven't yet given you a tour."

"Yes, it will only take a moment."

She slipped away, feeling a flood of relief pour over her shoulders. She rubbed her forehead. Only a few short minutes engulfed in such sociality had given her a headache. The men resumed their conversation behind her. She had only taken a few short paces when she heard a piece of the conversation that stopped her, clutching her back with ice. A simple name.

"Miss Eleanor Claridge."

Amelia whirled around before realizing that she should be acting nonchalant. Lord Ramsbury's back faced her, and he leaned toward his friend. She couldn't be certain if Lord Ramsbury had spoken the name of Mr. Claridge's sister, or if it had been his friend, Mr. Vane. Before she could be caught eavesdropping, she ducked behind a group of women that passed, following their steps to a nearby wall. She strained her ears, unable to hear from such a distance. Lord Ramsbury and Mr. Vane appeared to be speaking in hushed tones. Lord Ramsbury cast his eyes around, as if to avoid being heard. Amelia's heart pounded in her chest.

"Miss Buxton?" His eyes found her standing near the wall.

Her breath caught in her throat. She had been discovered. She feigned interest in her skirts, brushing unseen dirt from them. "Lord Ramsbury!" she laughed. "I forgot the way out of the assembly room."

He cocked his head to the side, raising a finger directly in front of where Amelia was standing. The door stood in clear view. The smirk on his face made her skin itch with annoyance.

"Oh! How could I have missed it? Thank you." She picked up her skirts to speed her walk as she made her way to the door. Her legs shook. What did Lord Ramsbury know about Eleanor's disappearance? That whispered conversation had been more than a chat about horses, politics, and the seasonal hunt, or whatever it was that men conversed about.

"Aunt Margaret!" Amelia half-whispered as she approached her aunt on the bench. She had fallen asleep, her mouth hanging open and her thick curls tucked under her chin as a cushion. Amelia shook her aunt's shoulder.

Aunt Margaret's eyes flew open and she snorted, wiping a string of drool from her cheek. "Have you woke me to announce your engagement?" With great effort, she pushed herself to better posture, fully awake and ready to devour every detail.

"No, and I never shall pursue that pompous man. Certainly not after what I now suspect him of." Amelia swallowed.

Aunt Margaret leaned forward. "What is it?"

"I heard him mention Eleanor Claridge's name."

Her brow scrunched. "Who?"

"The sister of the man we met this morning at the shore."

Aunt Margaret's face contorted in focus before she gasped. "Oh, yes! The missing girl?"

"Indeed. I witnessed Lord Ramsbury and an acquaintance of his in a hushed conversation of which Eleanor's name was mentioned. I'm afraid that's all I heard." Amelia chewed the nail of her index finger. She needed to inform Mr. Claridge. But how would she find him?

"Now, Amelia, you mustn't worry yourself over this.

Perhaps with our dip in the morning your mind will become clear."

Amelia sighed. Perhaps her aunt was right. Amelia already had plenty to worry about without becoming too involved in the mystery of the missing Claridge girl. It was likely that Mr. Claridge would find the information he sought in his conversation with Eleanor's friend, Miss Darby. She hoped he did. Amelia had been unable to cast the sorrowful blue eyes of Mr. Claridge out of her mind all day. With the urgency he had left them at the water's edge, Amelia was almost certain that he would have met with Miss Darby by this afternoon.

"Now," Aunt Margaret said, "Shall we explore the path near the royal pavilion? I should like to try to sketch it." She fetched her cane and stood, filled with energy once more.

As it were, Amelia would love a distraction, an activity that didn't involve husband hunting. One day in Brighton and she was already tired of trying. If only she didn't have such a firm time limit. She wanted to enjoy her time in Brighton as much as she could, without the worry of ending her time here without a fiancé. Her stomach turned with regret that she had ever agreed to such a thing. Amelia had rarely seen a happy marriage for herself, least of all between her parents. She knew it was impossible. She pushed the worry from her heart for the moment. At least she could enjoy visiting the royal pavilion. With a smile, she faced Aunt Margaret. "That sounds lovely."

Chapter 7

Miss Darby lived on the corner where Adam's own neighborhood transitioned to the fishing village. Hers was the last house before a string of cottages, positioned like a large cat looming over a family of mice. Adam tried to clear his mind as he walked. He needn't accuse her of being dishonest simply because Miss Amelia had suspected it. Why he had even taken any of Miss Amelia's words to heart was a mystery to Adam.

When he reached the doorstep of the Darbys' home, he lifted the knocker and struck the door three times. The butler allowed him entrance, smiling warmly. Adam fiddled with the fob on his waistcoat as he waited to enter the drawing room where Miss Darby sat. He was prepared to study her reaction to his visit, just as Miss Amelia had suggested.

The door opened and Adam entered, lifting his eyes to meet Miss Darby's as she stood. Her younger sister, Mary, stood beside her, positioned in front of the sofa directly across from him. Much like the last time he had visited, sunlight poured through the crimson drapery, falling upon both ladies in an angelic manner.

"Good day, Miss Darby, Miss Mary." He paused to observe Miss Darby's hands wringing together, her mouth pinched tight. Her eye contact faltered as Adam studied her face, searching for clues there. Miss Mary smiled in greeting, much like what Adam would have expected of Miss Darby. . .if she hadn't anything to hide from him.

"I am sorry to intrude on your hospitality." He walked into the room, stopping at the settee and taking a seat. The women reclaimed their seats on the sofa without a sound.

"It is not an intrusion, Mr. Claridge," Miss Mary said in a cheerful voice.

"I am glad to hear it." His eyes shifted to her elder sister. "I have come to speak with you, Miss Darby, once again, about my sister Eleanor."

"Oh?" Her brow rose. She scooped up her large orange cat from her feet, setting it on her lap, avoiding Adam's eyes. The cat watched him, its green eyes unblinking.

"She is still missing," Adam said.

"Oh, dear." Miss Darby stroked her cat. The animal squirmed, jumping off her lap and racing out the drawing room door behind him. Finding herself without a distraction, Miss Darby picked up a small book from the tea table and leafed through the pages. "I do hope she is well." Her voice shook, but not with emotion. When she glanced up, he saw nothing in her eyes that showed she feared for Eleanor's safety.

"I wondered if you knew anything else . . . anything at all, about where she might be. You were the last person to have seen her." Adam's heart pounded as he awaited her reply. He knew Miss Darby had claimed to not have seen Eleanor that day. But he was testing her memory. Facts were often easier to remember than lies.

Miss Darby glanced up from the book. "Yes, and I dearly wish I could see her again."

It seemed he had caught her. "What was she wearing that day? Do you recall?"

"Her rose taffeta gown. She looked beautiful."

Adam felt a familiar chill on his neck. "You told me previously that you did not see Eleanor that day. You told me she never arrived for your walk."

Miss Darby snapped her book shut, setting it on her lap. Her eyes widened, but she tried to hide her regret over her words. Eleanor had indeed been wearing a rose gown that day, Adam had a faint memory of the skirts catching in the door as she departed that evening of her disappearance. But Miss Darby had seen her. Why had she originally made a claim to the contrary?

Adam sat forward, fixing Miss Darby with a look of stone. "I require that you tell me everything you know. Now."

She swallowed. "I know nothing."

"Eleanor could be dead! Does that mean nothing to you?" The harshness of Adam's voice made tears spring to Miss Darby's eyes. He found it odd that she chose this moment to cry rather than the moment he had informed her of Eleanor's disappearance. His voice softened. "Please, if you care for her at all, tell me what you know. It could help me bring her home."

Miss Darby breathed out a long stream of air, dabbing at the corners of her eyes with a handkerchief.

"Excuse me, Mr. Claridge. It is time you took your leave," a deep voice said from the doorway.

Adam looked to see the Mr. Darby standing there, a deep scowl in his brow. The man stood at least three inches taller than Adam's already tall frame, with broad shoulders and a large jaw. Miss Darby stood in a flutter of fabric, rushing to her father's outstretched arms. She wept into his shoulder and he patted her blonde curls.

Adam gritted his teeth, but complied, standing with a nod. "Please accept my sincere apology, Miss Darby. I did not intend to . . . disturb you so greatly."

She sniffed, but kept her face hidden. Adam suspected the reason to be that the tears she flaunted were entirely fake. Adam passed Mr. Darby and walked out the door, forcing himself to keep from telling the man that his daughter was a liar.

"You are not welcome here again, Mr. Claridge." Mr. Darby said in an unrelenting voice.

Adam nodded in the awkward silence, taking his leave before Mr. Darby could force him out.

The fresh outdoor air did not remove Adam's anxiety. He walked with long strides, eager to return home to see that his father was well. It ached him to know that he had nothing of value to report regarding Eleanor. His father would likely be disappointed.

How was Miss Darby involved? What secrets was she keeping? He felt helpless. Mr. Darby would never let Adam call upon his daughter again. How could Adam discover what he needed to know? A great knot of despair replaced the anger stirring in his heart. He needed help. His mind traveled to Miss Amelia and her aunt. He recalled the elder Miss Buxton saying that she would be visiting the dippers in the morning. Surely Miss Amelia would be there too. As much as he would hate asking for her assistance again, he needed it. Now, more than ever. If he hoped to find Eleanor he needed the mind of a woman, but more than that, he needed a woman to act as his spy.

Riding in a sedan chair was not an experience Amelia wished to repeat. Aunt Margaret's chair was being carried ahead. Amelia followed in her own sedan chair from behind, a small enclosed contraption with one seat inside and no wheels, relying on the men carrying it on both sides to keep it in motion. Amelia watched the men carrying Aunt Margaret as they struggled to keep her balanced. She felt the imbalance of her own contraption as she was carried up a steep and possibly treacherous hill. Suppose they dropped her? Her stomach lurched. She closed her eyes and laughed, all alone in her sedan chair. She had gotten herself into a terrible plight.

At last Amelia watched as Aunt Margaret's chair was placed on solid ground. Being early enough in the day, not many people were out. Amelia thanked the heavens that there would be few witnesses to her embarrassment. She wanted her shame to be witnessed by as few people as possible.

When her own feet touched the sandy ground, she nearly bent over and kissed it. Aunt Margaret hobbled over to her, the early morning breeze twisting tendrils of hair into her face. "I feel quite like the queen!"

Amelia laughed. She had to admit, it had indeed felt fairly queen-like to be carried in such a way.

"I wonder if the Prince Regent has been carried in one of these very chairs," Aunt Margaret mused. "Would that not be tremendous?"

"Very tremendous," Amelia said.

Aunt Margaret stretched her leg, rubbing it at the hip. "How quickly do you suppose the cure will take its effect?" Her eyes brimmed with excitement and hope. Amelia was not one to think of hope in a negative way, but when hope was placed in such a hopeless thing...the result could be painful.

Amelia smiled. "I haven't the slightest idea. Perhaps our dipper will know."

"Ah! You are right. I shall ask her."

Amelia looked out at the ocean, swaying with tiny waves, brewing with bubbles and foam, and was suddenly struck with fear. What sort of creatures could be swimming about under the surface? She swallowed against her nerves. Despite the negative, was glad she was doing this. She may not have fully believed in the cure of the Brighton waters, but she did want to experience every excitement that Brighton had to offer during the short time she was here. And that certainly included taking a dip.

Two tall wooden 'bathing machines' were parked a distance away on the beach, swaying in the shallow water that spilled over the sand. Aunt Margaret had explained to Amelia that bathing machines were a method of privacy when changing into dipping clothes. One could enter the bathing machine, change into dipping clothes behind wooden walls, be dipped, and return to the machine and change back to your dry dress, all there floating on top of the water. The men were bathed in the east of the Brighton coast, and didn't care for such privacy. She reminded herself never to venture to the east shore during dipping hours.

Despite the modesty of the bathing machines, Amelia did not fancy the idea of being in such confines while floating in the middle of the ocean. Her throat grew dry with fear.

"Shall we go? The dipper is awaiting us!" Aunt Margaret led the way to the two bathing machines that awaited them. Tall and narrow, the wood appeared to be tightly constructed with a small door at the front. Amelia studied it, hoping that not a single drop of water would seep through the wood.

A pair of robust women held the ends of a rope out in the water that attached to the bathing machines, waiting to draw them farther into the ocean. Amelia could hardly contain her shock at the two women. The first woman, large and sturdy, appeared to have planted her own head upon a man's shoulders. Her broadness and muscle could only be explained by her chosen occupation. The other woman, also robust, looked to be quite elderly. Both women wore clothes similar to those that Amelia would soon be wearing.

"Do you have my dipping clothes?" Amelia asked.

Aunt Margaret scowled. "Only my own."

"You did not bring mine?" Just that morning Aunt Margaret had told Amelia that she would be packing her dipping clothes with her own.

"It seems I forgot to fetch yours." Aunt Margaret shrugged her shoulders.

Amelia's eyes widened. What was she to do without dipping clothes? She refused to dip in the chosen method of the men of Brighton.

Aunt Margaret climbed inside her own machine, closing the door behind her. A short woman opened the door from within Amelia's machine smiling in greeting. She reached out a hand to Amelia, pulling her to the step that led inside.

"A fine morning, is it not?"

Amelia did not consider this to be a fine morning at all.

"In you go." The woman pulled Amelia inside, closing the door to the bathing machine behind them. Surrounded by darkness, Amelia couldn't help but panic. She tried to calm her breathing, but only made it worse as she tried to stand perfectly centered in the machine to avoid rocking more than necessary. *Aunt Margaret didn't have her dipping clothes?* Amelia could not enter the water in her gown! It was made of fine muslin and edged in white Vandyke points. The lace would no doubt discolor in the sea water.

The woman pulled open a small hatch on one wall to let in fresh air and enough light to see. Amelia stepped carefully toward it. She saw Aunt Margaret's bathing machine pull away from the shore, floating out in front of her. Seconds later, the hatch on Aunt Margaret's machine opened, and her face appeared there, smiling over at her.

"What am I to do about my bathing clothes?" Amelia tried to hide the panic in her voice.

Aunt Margaret called out to her across the water, and Amelia could almost hear her say it before she did. "I suppose you'll be bathing nude after all!"

Amelia could hardly endure the terror that clutched her. She would *not*.

"I have your dipping clothes here, miss." The woman's voice came from behind Amelia, making her jump.

"For me?"

"Yes, of course. Your aunt sent them in preparation for your dip this morning."

Relief flooded through Amelia and she cast a glare at her aunt across the water. Aunt Margaret threw her head back in laughter, the maniacal sound nearly lost in the vastness of the surrounding ocean.

"If only you had seen the look of horror on your face." Aunt Margaret snorted as Amelia's machine floated closer.

Her face split into a reluctant smile as the maid assisted her in changing. She wiped the perspiration off her palms onto the strange white sheet she seemed to be wearing. She did not hate it as much as she thought. At least she would be wearing *something*.

"I hope you find the Brighton waters to be most invigorating, miss." The maid opened the door, gesturing to the water below.

Amelia gave a shaky laugh. "I suspect they shall be." Her eyes caught on the dipper that had been assigned to her. It was the elderly woman, smiling up at her with a somewhat toothless grin. "Good mornin,' miss!"

Amelia sat down on the edge of her bathing machine, dipping only the lower half of her legs in the sea water. Chill bumps spread over her legs as the salty water traveled up them. Her heart thumped. "How deep is the water here?" She eyed the woman that would be dipping her. She must have been at least six inches taller than Amelia.

The dipper shrugged. "I'd give a fair estimate, that it's only deep 'nough to reach your shoulders."

Amelia swallowed. The water was very cold. She inhaled deeply and held it as she lowered herself into the water. Trusting the old woman, Amelia let go of the bathing machine step, expecting to feel the seafloor under her toes. But her feet didn't hit the sandy bottom until her head was completely submerged. She kicked off the wet sand, sputtering out the water that filled her nose. Her eyes blinked out the salty water that streamed down from her hairline. Her lungs burned.

"You can't be dippin' yourself, miss," the woman grumbled, pulling Amelia closer by the arm. "What's ailing you this mornin'?"

"Nothing," she choked.

"Oh, there must be something! Do you waste my time?"

Amelia coughed, rubbing her nose. "No . . . well, I suffer from . . . worry. Anxiety and fear as well, I'm afraid." She spoke of the requirement her father had placed upon her. The fear she spoke of was born of the prospect of marrying Mr. Clinton. It seemed she was ailing from many things.

The dipper frowned, two deep wrinkles taking over her forehead. "Why d'you suffer these things?"

Amelia considered keeping it a secret, but something told her this woman would not relent until she was told. And Amelia wanted to escape the water as soon as possible. As she considered it, she realized it would be a relief to share her burden with a stranger. "My father requires me to become engaged to a man in Brighton within these summer months." She puffed a breath, struggling to keep her head above a passing wave. "Otherwise he has a man chosen for me to marry that I do not love."

The woman clicked her tongue. "A true ailment, indeed. You'll need a prescribed twenty dips."

"Twenty?" Amelia gasped.

She could barely speak before the woman lifted her by the waist, lowering her into the water with great force. Amelia gasped for air as she came up, only to be lowered again. What felt like an eternity later, Amelia was at last released from the woman's surprisingly strong arms. She scrambled into the bathing machine, blinking the salt water from her eyes.

She surveyed the area, sitting on the edge of the bathing machine to catch her breath. She burst into laughter as she saw Aunt Margaret being lifted and lowered repeatedly into the water. Had Amelia truly just experienced that for herself? It was positively ridiculous. Yet tourists flocked here to these waters by the hundreds.

"You'll begin to see the effects of the cure immediately," The dipper promised with a toothless smile.

Amelia didn't believe a word of it, but thanked her before allowing the maid in the bathing machine to help her back into her dry gown. Through the small window of the machine, Amelia could see the nearby coast behind her and the throngs of women that had begun to gather there, awaiting their turn to enter the bathing machine in which Amelia stood. She wished she could warn them all that the Brighton waters held no cure, only a madwoman that quite enjoyed nearly drowning people.

Amelia froze, her attention catching on something on the beach among the crowd of women. A man, tall, dark, standing aside from the group. She squinted. Could it be Mr. Claridge? No. He could not see her here and know that she had just been dipped. Worst of all, she secretly agreed with him—the waters were nothing more than a foolish legend, but she had convinced him that she did believe in them.

As Amelia considered her current condition, she realized she did indeed feel much more invigorated. Perhaps the cure did hold some truth. Repeatedly splashing into cold water was known to awaken the senses. She attributed that to the reason why Mr. Claridge appeared even more handsome than before, standing on the coastline in a dark jacket and green waistcoat.

When Aunt Margaret's dipping was complete, she met Amelia at the shore. Amelia touched her hair, self-conscious of the soaking mess it must have been. She did not want to imagine the state of her appearance.

"Mr. Claridge is here," Amelia half-whispered to her

aunt. She remembered that she still needed to tell him about what she had overheard at the assembly room with Lord Ramsbury, speaking in that secretive way with the soldier, Mr. Vane.

"Why the devil is he dawdling about this side of the coast?" Aunt Margaret cast a disapproving look at Mr. Claridge.

Amelia did not know. She forced a smile upon her face as the boat stopped and they stepped out onto the sand. Mr. Claridge stood with his arms crossed over his chest, a serious look stretched over his face. If only he could smile more. Amelia had only seen one smile of his in their first meeting, and she had been overwhelmed to say the least. A man with a smile as perfect as his ought to never let it leave his face. It was strange . . . he did not seem surprised to see Aunt Margaret and Amelia walking toward him. It was as if he had been expecting them.

"Miss Buxton, Miss Amelia, I thought I might find you here." Mr. Claridge nodded in their direction, his gaze locking on Amelia's. Amusement flickered in his eyes. "I see you have taken a dip."

"And I feel most invigorated," Amelia said, raising her chin. Why she felt the need to defend the cure so firmly was a mystery to her. "I daresay it is already taking effect."

Aunt Margaret stretched, smiling with satisfaction as she rubbed her leg. "Ah, yes. The pain is much less intense than before."

Amelia nodded in agreement. Mr. Claridge pressed his lips together, keeping that smile hidden—likely with the sole intent to taunt her. "Are you certain?"

"I am," Aunt Margaret said. "Why do you not take a dip, Mr. Claridge?" She seemed to have forgotten her dislike of him, for her question sounded genuine. "I suspect you would enjoy it very much."

He raised a skeptical eyebrow. "I could never be daft enough to do such a thing."

Amelia scowled. She had blamed his rudeness on his circumstances before, but it now seemed that his lack of manners was inherent.

"Are you so bold as to call my niece and me daft?" Aunt Margaret asked with a look of disgust.

"In this instance, yes."

His stony expression and snide remarks had begun to irk Amelia. She took a step closer to him, catching his gaze. "I must agree with my aunt. I insist you take a dip, Mr. Claridge. Perhaps it might cure you of your disagreeable personality."

The look of shock on his face satisfied Amelia more than she cared to admit. It was her turn to hide her smile as she stepped around him. "Let us return home, Aunt Margaret," she said over her shoulder. She wanted to help Mr. Claridge, but not if he continued insulting her.

A strong hand caught her by the elbow, stopping her. She looked up at Mr. Claridge, willing herself to keep an unyielding expression.

He released her elbow, his blue eyes pinching with regret. "You are right. I have forgotten my manners."

"Perhaps you might find them in the water," Aunt Margaret piped in.

Amelia couldn't stop her smile. She looked down at her boots in an effort to hide it from Mr. Claridge. But when she looked up again, he smiled too. She cursed her grin for widening at the sight of his.

"If I had a moment to spare in search of my manners, I certainly would, but I'm afraid I have another search demanding my time."

His search for Eleanor. "Have you any new knowledge?" Amelia asked. Her curiosity couldn't be helped.

"No, I'm afraid not. I spoke with Miss Darby, but she would not reveal any secret to me. Her father demanded that I leave and never return. But I am almost certain Miss Darby knows more than she is revealing. You were correct."

"Oh, dear." Amelia bit her lip. It was a difficult situation. If he could not speak to her, how would he ever learn of the secrets she was hiding?

"I must thank you for your keen sense," he said. "I would not have suspected anything of Miss Darby without your insightful remarks." He hesitated, locking Amelia's gaze in his again. "Have you found any success in your search?"

"My search?" Amelia scowled in confusion.

"For a husband."

Against her will, she felt her cheeks burn. Drat. Why had Aunt Margaret ever mentioned such a despicable thing to him? "I have only spoken to one man here besides you." Lord Ramsbury's flirtatious smile flashed in her mind. She needed to tell Mr. Claridge what she had overheard at the assembly room. "His name was Lord Ramsbury. Miss Darby may not be our only source of information," she said. "In the time I spent with Lord Ramsbury I overheard a suspicious conversation. Do you know him?"

Mr. Claridge's expression soured. "Yes, I know him. I cannot say I am fond of him."

"Nor am I." Amelia shook her head with vigor.

"But he is quite fond of you," Aunt Margaret said with a chuckle.

"Indeed. But what I mean to say is that he may know something of Eleanor's disappearance." Amelia relayed the exchange she had witnessed to Mr. Claridge, adding that she hadn't been able to hear the remainder of the two men's conversation.

His eyes hardened. "I remember a ball held near the pavillion last month. Lord Ramsbury had claimed the waltz with Eleanor. She had been quite smitten with his flattery."

Of course. Amelia knew Lord Ramsbury's compliments were not unique to her. He was a flirt of the worst kind. She hoped never to see him again.

"Thank you for telling me," Mr. Claridge caught her gaze, holding it to emphasize his words. The sorrow still hung in his eyes, but it was mingled with hope. "You may be of greater assistance to me than I originally expected." He rubbed his jaw, as if considering his next words carefully. "I came here to ask one favor of you. But now I would venture to ask two favors of you."

Amelia eyed him with misgiving. She could see by the hunch of his shoulders that he didn't enjoy asking for her help. "Would you like to borrow my intelligence again?" she asked. "It is not free of charge, you know."

A light smile touched his lips and he crossed his arms. "What is your price?"

"Ten-thousand pounds."

He chuckled, a deep and genuine sound. "Perhaps I should seek help from your aunt instead."

Aunt Margaret threw him a scowl. "I would not help you for twenty-thousand pounds and a new leg."

Amelia gasped, covering her mouth to hide the laughter that followed. Aunt Margaret pressed down her smile, throwing Mr. Claridge a wink. Even she could not stay angry with him for long.

"What is it that you ask?" Amelia said.

He sighed. "Considering that I am no longer welcome to enter the Darby household, and Miss Darby failed to give me the information I seek, I will need to find it through another source."

Amelia narrowed her eyes. "And what source do you speak of?"

"You."

"Me?"

"I would ask that you befriend Miss Darby. Keep your acquaintance with me a secret, and speak with her as a friend in order to gain her trust. Perhaps she then might confide in you."

A surge of excitement filled Amelia at the thought of being such a spy. It would add to the adventure of Brighton, but it would also take much of her time that she needed to be devoting to husband hunting. She puzzled over how to respond.

"There is the other favor…" Mr Claridge seemed even more reluctant to ask this one. Apprehension tightened in Amelia's chest as he inhaled to speak. "I would ask that you further your acquaintance with Lord Ramsbury."

Amelia's eyes widened.

She tried to protest, but Mr. Claridge added in a quick voice, "If he knows anything at all, I would be the last person he would inform, considering that I am Eleanor's brother. It is entirely possible that he is dangerous, so I shall be present during every meeting you have with him, keeping myself hidden, but available should you need protection."

Further her acquaintance with Lord Ramsbury? Could anything be less desirable? She could not endure endless conversations that held nothing but insincere flattery. She would have to pretend she enjoyed his company. Mr.

Claridge asked too much of her. She remembered that she was supposed to be seeking out an engagement here in Brighton. She could not make it appear that she was attached to Lord Ramsbury while she was seeking to secure an engagement elsewhere. It would not work.

"I know we have just met, Miss Amelia, but I am in desperate need of your help. I believe I can trust you." He begged her with is eyes.

"The price for that service might have to be twenty thousand pounds, after all," Amelia said in a weak voice. "I do wish to help you, but such a task would render my own search impossible. I cannot meet many gentlemen if I am forming a false attachment to Lord Ramsbury."

Mr. Claridge's mouth tightened in a frown. He examined Amelia's face for several seconds, making her feel quite vulnerable under his penetrating blue eyes. "I may be speaking too freely, so please correct me if I am. But why do you seek a husband here in Brighton? And why so urgently?" he said.

She exchanged a look with Aunt Margaret, who simply nodded, urging her to tell him. She swallowed hard. "It is a pathetic story. What I did. . .it was not very intelligent of me."

"I am not surprised," Mr. Claridge teased, half his mouth lifting in a smile.

Amelia rolled her eyes. "The town I have lived in all my life is crowded and boring and dull. I longed to escape, and after reading much about Brighton in the *Times,* it became something of a dream. My father did not wish to allow me the trip, for he is worried that I will never marry. So he allowed me the trip for a price. He is a man of preparation and has little belief in love, so he has chosen a dreadful man from Nottingham for me to marry, should I not return from Brighton engaged." Amelia sighed. "But I have no desire to marry a man I do not love."

Mr. Claridge was silent for a long moment. "As I understand it, your father did not specify that you had to *marry* another man, or otherwise marry this 'dreadful man.' He only specified that you had to be engaged."

Amelia paused. "Yes."

Mr. Claridge drummed his fingers on his leg, deep concentration in his features. "If you will agree to assist me in finding Eleanor, I offer you my assistance in return."

"How so?"

"Should the time come that you are to return home, and have yet to find a man you could love, I will act the part."

Amelia eyed him with suspicion, tilting her head to the side. "You will pretend to be engaged to me?"

"Yes. In your father's eyes, we will be engaged in every way. You will have fulfilled your end of the bargain. At that point, we may do one of three things: End the engagement in a proper fashion, falsify my death, or marry."

Amelia puzzled over his words. "I think I would prefer the first option."

"That is understandable."

Her heart raced with hope. His offer was tempting. She would have no need to worry over courting and flirting and sociality. She could enjoy her time in Brighton, help Mr. Claridge find Eleanor, and stay true to her word to her father—in a way. It still felt oddly devious to become engaged with the intent to simply end it. But it was true, her father had only said she had to be *engaged*. Of course her marriage had been an unspoken part of their arrangement, but she had only shaken his hand upon the spoken arrangement.

Mr. Claridge took a step closer. "You should never be forced to be a bride to a man you do not love. I will do everything I can to help you avoid such a fate."

She dared a glance at his face. Sincerity showed in every shade of blue in his eyes, every line of his expression. Her heart skipped and she scolded it for doing so. "But that does not change the fact that I will be forced to be in the company of Lord Ramsbury."

Mr. Claridge did not break her gaze. "Please, Miss Amelia. I would not ask if I were not desperate for information."

Aunt Margaret, who had been standing in uncharacteristic silence, stepped forward. "You cannot refuse, Amelia. Think of the convenience of the arrangement. You will be free to do with your time here what you wish. Lord Ramsbury will not require much coercing. He was so smitten with you he would reveal any secret you ask of him. Mr. Claridge does not ask for much in return."

A convenient engagement, indeed. One with no stipulations or future commitment. An engagement without a marriage attached. Amelia's face spread into a slow smile. She extended her hand to Mr. Claridge. "It seems we have a bargain of our own."

He smiled without reservation, taking her hand gently in his.

A shiver edged over her spine as she felt her worry and anxiety fade away. She squinted out at the ocean where her dipper stood in the waves. The dipper's claim that Amelia would be cured of her worry had just come to pass, right before her eyes.

Perhaps the cure was real after all.

"What is wrong?" Mr. Claridge released Amelia's hand.

She grinned up at him, laughing with disbelief. "I've

been cured by the Brighton waters!" She covered her mouth in shock.

He gave her a quizzical look.

"I've been cured! It's all true."

Mr. Claridge blew out a long puff of air, raising his eyebrows. "Please do not ramble about the cure with Miss Darby, she may consider you mad and force you out of her home."

"Well, then you should have specified in our bargain that I could not mention the cure." Amelia raised her chin in defiance.

He laughed. "If you are to be my fiancé, I must somehow place a little sense in you."

"That I agreed to be your fiancé at all has already proven that I lack sense."

Aunt Margaret choked on a bout of laughter, leaning over on her cane. "Do not engage Amelia in a verbal sparring. She will always win, Mr. Claridge."

"I am beginning to see that." He stared down at Amelia, a certain fascination in his eyes. She looked down, embarrassed by the attention. She did not mean to be so outspoken, but Mr. Claridge had a way of bringing out the unrefined in her.

"Who shall I see first?" Amelia asked. "Miss Darby or Lord Ramsbury?" She wanted to get straight to work. The sooner she could help Mr. Claridge the sooner she could free herself of all responsibilities and enjoy the liberty of Brighton and her future of spinsterhood. Her mind soared with visions of traveling the world, seeing France, Scotland, India—the list could extend forever. But for now, finding Eleanor was paramount.

"Find Lord Ramsbury first," Mr. Claridge said. "You have already met. It will be easier."

Amelia had hoped he wouldn't say that.

"I will leave for the largest assembly room this evening at eight. The evening is the most likely time that he will be in attendance. Come shortly after me so we are not seen together. I will observe your interactions with him from a distance."

"He is not going to abduct me in the middle of a crowd, if that is what you are suggesting. I will be perfectly safe." Amelia didn't like the idea of Mr. Claridge witnessing the embarrassing flirtations that would likely be poured upon her. What Amelia dreaded most was acting as if they didn't bother her.

Mr. Claridge shook his head with firmness. "I wish to come. If you do discover that he was involved in Eleanor's disappearance, I need to be near enough to clobber him."

"He is right," Aunt Margaret said. "You cannot deny the man of a good clobbering, Amelia."

"Very well," she sighed. "But Lord Ramsbury mustn't see you there or he will never dare speak of your sister."

"I will be careful."

Amelia shivered as a gust of wind brought a salty mist of seawater against her back. The sun had only begun to fully rise for the morning, leaking its warmth and brightness down upon them. Mr. Claridge stepped backward, landing himself in a ray of sunlight that only intensified the color of his eyes. "I must thank you again for your willingness to assist me."

"And I must thank you for offering me such a convenient proposal."

Mr. Claridge's lips twitched into a smile. "Thank you for accepting it." He started to turn around, but stopped. "I must tell you, it is a ball that the assembly rooms are hosting this evening. I'm certain a man like Lord Ramsbury would not miss an opportunity of the sort. I will see you there shortly after eight."

Amelia had little time to comprehend his words before he started retreating down the coast. A ball? She would have to dance with Lord Ramsbury! At least he could not compliment her dancing without proving himself a liar. Dancing had never been a talent of hers.

She exhaled, long and slow to calm her nerves, turning to her aunt.

"I must own I thought it would take you much longer to find a fiancé." Aunt Margaret melted into a deep chuckle. "I cannot wait to see your father's expression when he learns you have tricked him."

"He will never learn. We are going to put an end to the engagement without telling Papa that it was all part of an elaborate plan."

"Or you could falsify Mr. Claridge's death. I quite liked that idea," Aunt Margaret mused.

Amelia laughed. "As did I. It is much more . . . romantic. My father would not press me to court any other man if I had just experienced such a devastation."

"Although the third option, marrying Mr. Claridge, would be most romantic of all, would it not?"

Amelia threw her a look of dismay. Aunt Margaret simply chuckled. "Come now, he is handsome at the very least."

"I knew that detail could not have passed your notice."

Aunt Margaret gave a devious grin. "Of course not. I'm not blind, you know."

Amelia laughed, her stomach stirring with excitement and nervousness. A pending false engagement to Mr. Claridge, a false courtship with Lord Ramsbury, and a false friendship with Miss Darby. How would she manage it all? Something was bound to go awry. She tried not to think too deeply on it as she linked her arm through her aunt's and returned to their house. She had a ball to prepare for.

Chapter 8

The ballroom was much too crowded for Adam's taste. He grimaced as group after group of people pushed through the door, flaunting their finest attire. He stood at the wall farthest from the music, hoping the absence of lit sconces around him would keep him hidden. He could see Lord Ramsbury, standing against the opposite wall, leaning his elbow against it as he sipped from a champagne flute. Adam stared at him, trying to decipher his character. Could such a pompous and careless man be involved in Eleanor's disappearance? He hoped Amelia could uncover the truth for him. He had placed a substantial amount of trust in her.

He thought of that morning, and the arrangement that had been made between them. He was unsure of what had compelled him to make such an offer. He was inviting her to deceive her father with his help. He had never known himself to be so dishonorable. Adam had been experiencing sharp pangs of guilt ever since leaving the coast that morning.

Sweeping his gaze over the crowd, he paused to check his pocket watch. It read half past eight. Amelia should have been there by now.

Growing anxious, Adam moved deeper into the corner of the room, keeping his eyes open and watchful of Lord Ramsbury as he waited. The man was utterly ridiculous. He dressed with the sole purpose of catching every eye in the room, giving them all devilish grins and brief greetings as if they were not worth his time. Unless they were privileged or beautiful, he did not care for their acquaintance. There was only one matter on which Adam agreed with Lord Ramsbury: Miss Amelia Buxton was worth pursuing. Since that morning Adam had struggled to clear his mind of her. She had agreed to risk so much to help him, nearly a stranger. He had never seen such devotion and kindness. He had glimpsed a side of her that intrigued him.

Not five minutes later, Miss Margaret Buxton stepped through the doorway of the ballroom, partially hidden behind a crowd of men. When he saw her fully, he could hardly contain his shock. She wore the most elaborate gown he had ever seen. She looked to have thrown herself into a seamstresses basket, picking up every matter of lace and trim imaginable. A turban adorned her head, complete with feathers and beads.

Distracted by the elder Miss Buxton's entrance, he failed to notice Miss Amelia's debut until she stepped out from behind her aunt.

His gaze lingered on her as she stood there, a shy smile on her lips, her skin glowing with radiance in the candlelight. She wore a simple blue gown, yet she stood out among dozens of extravagantly dressed women. Across the room, her eyes found his. He wanted to approach her, to ensure she knew what to say to Lord Ramsbury, but she just gave a discreet nod and immediately turned around to where Lord Ramsbury stood.

Adam watched as the elder Miss Buxton moved to a chair at the border of the room. Her niece would approach Lord Ramsbury alone.

Without a sound, Adam weaved through the thick crowd, stopping among another group of men where he would fit in unnoticed. He strained his ears to hear the beginning conversation between Ramsbury and Amelia.

Lord Ramsbury smiled as she approached, drinking her in with his eyes. "Miss Buxton. I worried I would never see you again. You look even more enchanting than I recall."

Adam gritted his teeth. How could any woman believe such heavy-handed flattery?

"And you are even more coquettish than I recall."

He laughed and she joined him. There was something in her laugh that was forced. Adam hoped it passed Lord Ramsbury's notice. A man in a top hat crossed Adam's view. He shifted past, struggling to hear the conversation.

"May I claim a place on your dance card this evening, Miss Buxton?"

"Of course you may."

"May I have the waltz?"

Adam watched as her posture tightened. "If you insist."

Lord Ramsbury leaned closer to her. "I certainly do insist. I insist upon the quadrille as well. Two dances, if I may."

"Very well." Her voice seemed to shake. Adam felt that familiar pang of guilt. Did she fear

Lord Ramsbury? It was Adam's fault that she was forced to interact with him at all. Her eyes flickered to him where he stood in the crowd. She looked away fast.

"I thought you would refuse," Lord Ramsbury said.

Amelia gave a bashful smile. "Why would I do that?"

"You did not seem to be very fond of me the last time we met. In fact, you seemed quite eager to escape my presence."

"Oh, I certainly was. I—er—felt ill. I suspect I might have vomited on your boots had I stayed a moment longer."

Adam caught a glimpse of her profile. She visibly cringed as the words escaped her lips. He pressed down a smile. Why did he find her awkward comments so charming? There was much about her he found charming, he realized. Too much.

Lord Ramsbury's expression lifted in surprise. "Well if that was indeed the case, I daresay I'm glad you left in such a rush. My boots are new, you know. I simply could not have you casting up your accounts upon them."

Amelia laughed, reaching out to touch his arm in a flirtatious way. "Perhaps it would have given your confidence a needed hit, my lord."

Adam clearly saw the insults through her words, but Lord Ramsbury seemed to take it all as teasing, or as encouragement. Amelia was more clever than he realized. She caught his eye again, and he could almost see her mind working.

"My aunt's leg ails her," she said to Lord Ramsbury. "She has chosen to sit rather than dance. I wish my dearest friend were here with me to enjoy the dances." She sighed in discontent.

"Where is this friend?"

"She has disappeared. She has been missing for weeks

now." Amelia looked down, rubbing her forehead. "I fear for her safety."

Adam watched Lord Ramsbury's expression carefully. There was a small twinge of recognition, of shock, but he masked it well. "How unfortunate . . . what is her name?"

"Eleanor Claridge." Amelia looked up, giving Lord Ramsbury a hopeful look. She touched his arm again, leaning closer. "Do you know her?"

Adam's heart thumped in anticipation. Lord Ramsbury had yet to give an answer. Adam slid farther into the crowd, closer to them, hoping to hear the answer more clearly.

"Do I see Adam Claridge?" A friendly voice asked from beside him. Adam recognized it instantly. Had it been anyone else, he might have ignored it. With great effort, he tore his gaze away from Amelia and Lord Ramsbury.

"By George, it is you!" Philip Honeyfield, a man Adam had known since his school years, slapped him on the shoulder. "It has been a year, at least, since I have seen you."

Adam smiled. Philip was one of the only people he could consider a trusted friend. His brown hair still fell in boyish curls over his forehead, just as it had ten years before at boarding school. His eyes, also brown, still carried the same open and innocent look.

Adam's eyes flickered to where Amelia stood before returning back to Philip. "I've simply been avoiding you, Honeyfield."

Philip threw his head back with a laugh, tightening his grip on Adams shoulder before releasing it. "I cannot say I believe that. But it would have been easy, given that I was not here. I've been traveling the continent the past year."

"Have you?" Adam asked, distracted. Lord Ramsbury had moved farther away with Amelia, now holding her hand in his, delivering a lingering kiss on top of it. Adam tried to hide his annoyance.

"Indeed. France has its wonders, but I must say that Brighton will always hold my heart." Adam hardly heard him. Amelia appeared to be feigning some sort of sadness, and Lord Ramsbury's attempts to console her were more than he could bear.

When he returned his attention to Philip, he realized he still wore a grimace. He quickly corrected his expression, but not before Philip noticed.

"Ramsbury claimed her attention before you, did he?"

Adam scowled. "Who?"

"The woman you have been unabashedly staring at. She is quite beautiful." Philip fixed his gaze on Amelia before throwing Adam a look of pity. "Accept your defeat gracefully, my friend. Ramsbury has a way of charming women that we ordinary men will never understand."

Adam laughed. Philip thought Adam fancied Amelia? How ridiculous. He shifted awkwardly. "I will never accept defeat from a man so pompous as Ramsbury."

"There it is! That is the attitude we all need. If you fancy her, devil take it, you pursue her!" Philip's voice roared loud in the air. Adam froze, hoping it wouldn't draw Lord Ramsbury's attention to him. He didn't know if he and Amelia were still speaking of Eleanor.

Philip's laughter subsided. "I like to hope I would have such courage. If ever a woman steals my heart, I will be bound to steal hers before any other man takes the chance."

Adam doubted Philip's words. He had always had a certain shyness about him where women were concerned.

The poor man could hardly keep his wits about him with a pretty lady nearby. But Philip had the kindest heart Adam knew. He hoped one day there would be a woman to see that.

"Ask her for a dance," Philip said when Adam's gaze crossed over to Amelia once again. "He cannot have claimed her entire dance card."

"He very well could have," Adam said.

Philip studied Lord Ramsbury as he flashed a smile at Amelia and combed his hand over his hair in one smooth motion. "I suppose you are right."

Couples around the room had begun to assemble in lines. The quadrille was soon to begin. Adam and Philip moved back against the wall. Adam had no interest in dancing and Philip was likely too terrified to ask for a partner.

Philip swallowed, putting on a look of nonchalance. "I do not particularly enjoy dancing."

"Nor do I," Adam said. He fixed his attention on Lord Ramsbury as he guided Amelia into the line. Amelia looked very much like Philip, terrified and uncomfortable, yet trying to hide it. The music began and Amelia's face turned the pale color of Lord Ramsbury's freshly starched cravat. She kept a significant distance between them throughout the dance, leaning away from him each time they came together. She stumbled once or twice, scowling at her feet instead of looking at her partner.

The dance ended, and Amelia looked as if she were about to collapse in relief. Her eyes met Adam's across the room, and her cheeks darkened to a pretty blush at the centers. He smiled to reassure her. Her lips lifted softly before Lord Ramsbury had her arm once again.

What had she discovered in their conversation? Had

Lord Ramsbury revealed anything about Eleanor? Adam needed to know.

"Philip," Adam turned to his friend. "May I ask for your assistance?"

"Always."

"I wondered if you might find yourself capable of distracting Lord Ramsbury for the course of one dance. Keep him away from Miss Buxton for me."

Philip laughed as if he thought Adam to be only jesting. His expression fell when he saw that Adam was not smiling. "How might I do that?" he scoffed.

"You have a clever mind, Honeyfield. You did always score higher than me in school."

Philip threw his head back in laughter. "That I did. Thank you for admitting your inferiority at last." He sneaked a glance at Lord Ramsbury before returning his gaze to Adam, eyes wide. "I shall give it my best attempt."

"I knew I could rely on you," Adam said.

Philip nodded, straightening his jacket before plunging into the crowd. Adam followed behind him from a distance of several feet, keeping close to the wall.

Philip stepped up beside Lord Ramsbury. The two were almost identical in height, but Lord Ramsbury exceeded Philip in breadth by several inches. After a moment of hesitation, Philip tapped Lord Ramsbury's shoulder. He seemed to shrink when Lord Ramsbury turned around.

"Good evening," Philip said. "There is an urgent matter of business that I must address with you privately." The urgency in his expression made Adam bite back a laugh.

Lord Ramsbury's brow furrowed in confusion. "What is it?"

"You do understand the meaning of the word *privately,*

do you not?" Philip nodded in the direction of the exit. "Please, it is an urgent matter indeed."

Adam watched as Lord Ramsbury whispered a quick explanation to Amelia and followed Philip across the room and out the door. What scheme Philip had planned Adam could only imagine. He hurried to Amelia, stopping behind her, observing the tension releasing from her shoulders.

"I would not have asked that you come to a ball if I had known how much you despise dancing."

Amelia rotated toward him, her face flushed. "What are you doing? Lord Ramsbury could return at any moment!" She glanced at the door.

"My friend will keep him away for long enough."

Amelia tilted her head to the side, making a straight strand of hair fall over her cheek. "I might have suspected you were involved in that odd display."

Adam had a strange urge to brush the hair off her face, to touch her blushing cheek. He stopped himself, realigning his expression to one of business instead of the admiration he worried she had seen. "I needed to speak with you. What have you discovered thus far?"

She sighed. "Not a great deal, I'm afraid. He did mention that he knew Eleanor. He stated, quite boastfully, might I add, that Eleanor fancied him. But he may be inclined to believe that every woman in the world fancies him, so I don't know how much credit to give his claim."

"Did he say anything else? Anything at all?"

"No. He seemed eager to change the subject of our conversation. I am almost certain there is more that he knows. He was taken by surprise when I mentioned her name."

Adam's mind spun, struggling to create theories. Eleanor would not have been foolish enough to pursue Lord Ramsbury. She had always acted aloof toward men of rank and title. Eleanor's opinion on marriage had always been to marry for love, to find a respectable, humble, and kind-hearted man. Lord Ramsbury did not seem to fit. Had Lord Ramsbury fancied Eleanor? He had danced the waltz with her at a ball before she disappeared. Had he hurt her because she hadn't returned his feelings? The idea shook Adam with anger. He pushed the thought away. He didn't have enough proof to let it shake him. Yet.

"It may take time to gain the information we seek," Amelia said. "Shall I meet with Miss Darby tomorrow? My efforts might be better spent with her."

"Yes, but you mustn't give up on Lord Ramsbury yet. I do not trust him."

Amelia sighed. "I do not know if he likes me enough to court me, but I suspect he would only confide in me if we were alone. Perhaps not even with a chaperone present."

Adam looked down at her brown eyes, wide with intent. He couldn't allow her to be alone with a man like Lord Ramsbury. Adam couldn't stomach the idea of Amelia being hurt or taken advantage of. He shook his head swiftly. "The waltz. You will be close enough to him to have a private conversation."

"I cannot ask him about Eleanor again tonight. He will realize my designs. I need to weave Eleanor carefully into our conversations." She waved her hands in the air. "With subtlety."

"We don't have time."

Amelia puffed out a breath of frustration. "How do you suggest I coerce the information from him then?"

He rubbed his chin, thinking. "You may start with giving him a proper dance."

Amelia gasped, planting her hands on her hips. "If you insult my dancing one more time, Mr. Claridge, I will—I will…refuse to ever enter an engagement with you."

He raised his eyebrows. "The engagement is in your favor, Miss Amelia. Not mine."

"Of course." She looked down at her gloves, pulling on the fingertips in silence.

The orchestra began a slow yet jovial interlude, and Adam extended his hand to Amelia. "Allow me to instruct you in a dance."

"Pardon me?" She cast her eyes about the room, panic overtaking her lovely features.

"If you wish to win over Lord Ramsbury, you will need to show him that you find him irresistible."

"I find him quite easy to resist, actually."

Adam chuckled, guiding her by the hand to the line of partners that had begun to form in the ballroom. The dance began and Amelia struggled through the steps, her cheeks deepening in color. "I'm a dreadful dancer," she breathed as she circled back to him around the other couples, stepping out of rhythm with the music. He didn't mean to laugh, but it escaped him nonetheless. He cleared his throat as she narrowed her eyes at him. She only held that expression for a moment before her lips twitched, splitting into a smile. "I cannot possibly charm Lord Ramsbury through my *graceful* dancing."

Adam took her hand, keeping her at arm's length as they turned. "You must convince him that you wish to be near him. He will trust you more if he sees that you trust him."

Adam hesitated before tugging gently on her small hand, bringing her nearer to him. Her elbow brushed over his as they turned. She looked down, a scowl marking her brow.

"You must smile at him," he said.

Her eyes flew up to his. "I cannot smile and dance at once. It requires more focus than I am capable of."

Adam grinned down at her. As if by magic, her smile followed, shrouding her entire face in beautiful light. "See, you've done it," he said. "You are more skilled than you think." Adam spotted a charming dimple near her mouth on the right side, deepened by the shadows the candlelight cast upon her. He swallowed, his heart suddenly crashing in his chest like a wave.

The dance brought her away from him for a moment, and she laughed at her missteps as she moved back toward him.

When the dance ended, Adam checked the entrance to the ballroom, remembering with regret why he was here. He had not come to dance with Amelia. He had come to find information that would lead him to Eleanor. A pang of guilt stabbed him once again. He couldn't let his focus slip.

Amelia inhaled deeply, her breathless giggles subsiding. "That was the first dance of my life I have not despised. You have proven yourself a very skilled partner."

Adam had never danced a more perfect dance in his life, despite the imperfections in Amelia's dancing. He puzzled over that for a moment. "Perhaps our false engagement will prove to be just as perfect a partnership as our dancing," he whispered.

She smiled up at him and he couldn't help but wonder if perhaps the engagement could become something more than a ruse. He would not entirely object. All at once, something seemed to shift in Amelia's expression. She lowered her eyes. "I never expressed my appreciation to you for offering such a thing. In truth, I never wish to marry." She looked up at him in gratitude. There was a certain sadness in her eyes, mingled with a firm resolve. "You have saved me from a fate I thought I could never escape."

Adam's heart sunk, but he tried to ignore it. Why was she so firmly against the prospect of marrying? He didn't want to think about why that bothered him so much, but with the way his heart wavered with her every word and smile, he had an inkling.

"Marriage? Is it such a cruel fate?"

She lifted her chin to look more directly at him. "I have never seen a happy one. And I am one who cannot fathom living unhappily."

Adam studied her expression, the uncertainty that flickered there as he took a step closer. "I believe a marriage can be the source of much happiness. Love and companionship are not to be discounted. What is a happy life without love?"

She sighed. "I cannot argue this matter with you, Mr. Claridge. Simply know my resolve is firm, and that I am forever grateful to you for offering me this engagement."

He nodded. There was more he wished to ask, but he could see in the solidity of her features that she would not answer if he did. All in a moment, barriers seemed to build between them, all comfort and ease banished. He cleared his throat. "Tomorrow at ten meet me at the place on the beach we first met. I will direct you to the residence of Miss Darby so you may begin your acquaintance with her."

She only met his eyes long enough to confirm their meeting with a nod, before an unwelcome voice broke the air.

"Miss Buxton, I'm sorry my business detained me for so long. Did I miss our waltz?"

Adam jumped a little, looking to his left where Lord Ramsbury stood.

"No, you have arrived just in time." Amelia turned her full attention to him, painting a smile onto her previously sullen expression.

Lord Ramsbury raised an eyebrow, studying Adam as if to evaluate his skill before a duel. "I see you have made a new acquaintance," Lord Ramsbury said to Amelia. His smile turned to Adam, dropping in increments. "Who might you be?"

"No person worth your time." Adam hardened his gaze before nodding and turning on his heel. He reclaimed his place on the outskirts of the ballroom, crossing his arms over his chest as he resumed his observation of Amelia and Lord Ramsbury from a distance.

Adam could not blame the man for being smitten with her, but he only hoped he didn't have wicked intentions. Amelia seemed to already house a distrust of men, a disbelief of love in a marriage. How could she believe something as ridiculous as the Brighton cure and not believe in love?

When the waltz began, Amelia took every piece of advice Adam had given her. She leaned toward Lord Ramsbury, smiled, and laughed. She was so skilled in her act, Adam wondered if it was even an act at all. His jaw tightened in jealousy as he turned his gaze away. He had not expected himself to hate this blasted arrangement so much.

If Lord Ramsbury didn't speak soon about Eleanor, Adam would have to take matters into his own hands. He couldn't have another man staring so longingly at *his* intended. Even if it was only a ruse.

Philip came through the ballroom door, a mischievous

grin on his face. He sneaked around the edge of the room before stopping beside Adam.

"Did I manage to detain him for long enough?" Philip asked, wiping a bit of perspiration from his forehead.

Adam laughed at the state of his friend. "Your timing was nearly perfect. How did you keep him away?"

"I convinced him his horses had been cut loose in his absence. He began calling them and searching for them without verifying my words." Philip chuckled. "Only much later did he realize they were still at his carriage. I hid myself behind the wheels of a tall phaeton."

Adam held back his laughter. "I would advise you to hide yourself again. If Lord Ramsbury discovers your trickery he might challenge you," he teased.

Philip's face lost a bit of color. "Are you quite serious?"

"I am always serious."

Philip seemed to puzzle over Adam's words before stepping farther into the corner of the room, tucking himself in the distance between two sconces where the light failed to reach.

"Are you afraid of Lord Ramsbury?" Adam asked.

"Not at all. I'm simply exercising caution." Philip looked back at where Lord Ramsbury and Amelia stood. His eyes widened before he threw Adam a look of disapproval. "What purpose did I have distracting him if you did not win the lady in his absence?"

"We danced," Adam said, only half-listening. He watched Amelia as she laughed at something Lord Ramsbury said.

"Then what is she doing over there?"

Adam tore his gaze from Amelia, giving Philip a half-hearted smile. "He must be a better dance partner than I ever will be."

"That deuced man," Philip whispered with a laugh. "He simply cannot fail."

Adam wondered if Lord Ramsbury's attention toward Amelia was genuine. If such were the case, he certainly *would* fail. What Lord Ramsbury didn't know was that Amelia would never marry him should he propose. She would never marry anyone.

Philip stepped out of his hiding place, gripping Adam's shoulder as if to console him. "Better fortune next time, my friend. I had best put an end to my evening festivities. I would hate to be the recipient of Lord Ramsbury's wrath. He seems to be skilled at achieving anything he pursues, and I suspect giving me a beating for my deceiving him would not be an exception."

Adam chuckled as he bid farewell to his friend, and resolved to keep a careful eye on Amelia for the rest of the evening. When the crowd had begun to disperse, he couldn't speak with Amelia, for Lord Ramsbury had offered her and her aunt a ride home in his carriage. So Adam took his walk home alone, enjoying the cool night air.

He kicked his boots on the path as he walked, frustrated now for more reasons than one. His sister was missing, his father was dying, and he was quickly forming an attachment to the woman that was meant to enter a false engagement with. He could never show her that he was beginning to view her as more than a brief acquaintance.

Dim light flickered in the windows of his home when it came into view. He entered, feeling his eyelids droop with fatigue. Rounding the corner to the hall, he found his father sitting in the library, his head resting on the bend of his elbow. A loud snore echoed in the empty room, bouncing off the shelves of the partially bare bookcases.

A tight knot of grief burned in Adam's throat. He swallowed it, carefully pulling out the chair opposite his father and sitting at the table without a sound. It was strange to see his father, a man he had always known to be strong, so weak and frail. The cycle of life was a cruel, unfair thing.

Adam's gaze focused on the deep crease of his father's forehead, shadowed by the nearby candle. The worry and grief for his daughter showed there in the crease, haunting him even as he slept. A surge of emotion struck Adam in the chest, and a tear slipped from his eye. Then another. He let them fall, undeterred by any watching eyes that expected him to be strong. What would he do without his father? He had spent so many hours focused on how to bring Eleanor home before his father died, without focusing on what he would do without a father. He would inherit the household, the land, the animals, everything. Alone. He would have no family left, especially if Eleanor was never found.

He stopped himself. She would be found. He could have nothing distract him now, and certainly not a woman that could never return his feelings. He couldn't let Amelia steal any more of his heart, or smiles, or attention. He stood, kissing his father lightly on the head before waking him and helping him to his bed. Tomorrow was a new day, and he knew exactly how he would spend it.

Chapter 9

"I'm in love! Can you believe it?" Aunt Margaret repeated the phrase for what seemed like the hundredth time since the night before. Amelia yawned, smiling up at her aunt from the sofa where she sat beside their maid, Fanny. The two exchanged a look of amusement as Aunt Margaret continued on about her 'one true love.' The woman had hardly paused to breathe between her exclamations of love for the man she had met the night before at the ball. Skeptical as she was, Amelia had offered her congratulations too many times to count. Now Aunt Margaret stood before her, still in her nightdress, hair comb in one hand, the other planted over her heart.

"Mr. Booth flirted with me all evening, Amelia."

"Did he?"

"Indeed. I daresay he will be calling upon me soon. He already expressed his interest in courting me."

Amelia lifted her brow. "I look forward to making his acquaintance."

"And you shall." Aunt Margaret combed through her curls, humming as she went. "I can hardly think of the pain in my leg. Mr. Booth has claimed all my attention."

Amelia chuckled as her aunt turned around, humming as she went. Amelia had never seen this Mr. Booth, for Aunt Margaret had claimed he retired for the night before she could escape Lord Ramsbury. Amelia wondered if Mr. Booth existed at all. Aunt Margaret had never been an advocate of love, but suddenly it was all she could speak of.

"You cannot possibly be in love already, Aunt Margaret. You have only just met the man," Amelia said, doubt creeping into her voice.

"Yes, but I admire him greatly. I feel he is in possession of a kindred soul to mine. Perhaps I am not in love with him yet, but I expect it should happen soon enough. I feel the beginnings of a stirring within my heart, a bird spreading its wings and longing to take flight."

Oh, dear. Her aunt had officially plummeted into madness. Amelia kept her mouth closed against her retort. When Aunt Margaret disappeared into her bedchamber, Fanny followed to assist her in dressing.

Amelia fell back on the cushions of the sofa, chewing the nail of her index finger. She had yet to tell Mr. Claridge that she had failed to discover anything else from her time with Lord Ramsbury. She smiled at the thought of the dance she and Mr. Claridge had shared. He had seemed a different man the night before than he had been on the beach. He smiled more, teased her, made her feel things she didn't recognize. She thought of the depth in his eyes, the width of his smile, and a stirring started in her heart. She froze.

It felt very much like a bird spreading its wings and longing to take flight.

"Amelia!"

She jumped off the sofa, as if her thoughts had somehow been overheard. "Yes?"

"When is our meeting with Miss Darby today? After my extensive conversation with Mr. Booth in the ballroom, I am eager for a lengthy conversation of the female variety. Men cannot discuss ribbons and lace, you know."

"We meet Mr. Claridge at the north beach at ten."

Her stomach turned with nervousness. She had never considered herself to be very skilled when it came to being social. But she would need to employ every skill in her arsenal in order to get the information from Miss Darby that Mr. Claridge required of her. Her confidence wavered as she stood up and moved to her bedchamber to get ready. She would need to appear fashionable and proper in order to gain a bit of Miss Darby's trust upon first glance. With Fanny's assistance, Amelia would style her hair as beautifully as she could. Perhaps Amelia would even come to Miss Darby with a basket of scones or tea cakes. She stopped herself. She had no scones or tea cakes. She could only come with an offering of false friendship.

How lovely.

When Aunt Margaret and Amelia had made themselves presentable, they hurried out the door with two minutes to spare. They rushed up the sandy bank to the proper location. Mr. Claridge was already there, arms crossed, dark hair creating a sharp contrast against the pale blue sky.

"Good morning, Mr. Claridge!" Amelia called out as they approached. He greeted them with a nod. No smile. Amelia quickly made her face to resemble his, embarrassed that she had been so friendly. This meeting was a matter of business, much like their relationship. But the night before had been different. Had it not?

"Miss Darby often took a morning walk with Eleanor and a woman named Miss Reed," Mr. Claridge said. "She and Miss Reed should be departing soon from the Darby residence. If your timing is correct, you should catch them as they set off toward the west shore."

Mr. Claridge's voice was cold and dull, much like it had been the first time they met here on the beach. What had happened to the friendly demeanor he had sported the night before? Amelia tipped her head to the side, trying to decipher what it could be.

"Very well, we shall leave now," Amelia said. She turned to Aunt Margaret, who nodded in agreement.

"I will need to direct you to her home," Mr. Claridge said. He seemed to be avoiding her eyes. "After you have finished speaking with Miss Darby, return here to relay what you heard."

Amelia scowled. Why was he acting so demanding and aloof? His posture was stiff and his mouth firm and flat, as if he were exercising a conscious effort to keep even a ghost of a smile at bay. It vexed her to no end. She had enjoyed the version of Mr. Claridge that had danced with her at the ball the night before. This was not the same man.

"As you wish," Amelia said, her own voice stern, dropping a curtsy. His eyes flicked to hers, and she cast him a questioning look before returning her attention to her aunt. "You must be polite in your words with Miss Darby. We cannot afford to offend her."

Aunt Margaret gasped. "Posh. I am always polite."

"If I may," Mr. Claridge interrupted. "I must attest from personal experience that you have just made yourself a liar." He made a sound—a small laugh.

Amelia's eyes shot to his. He looked away from her eyes, wiping the smile off his face as if it had never been there. Frustration boiled inside her. He would laugh with Aunt Margaret but not with her? Had she done something to offend him? She puzzled over every interaction they had shared the night before, but could think of nothing she might have done.

They began their walk toward the Darby residence, and Mr. Claridge remained aloof, keeping his mouth closed unless to make a quick remark to her aunt. He did not even spare Amelia a glance. Despite her effort to stop it, her heart stung as if she had lost a dear friend. What had happened to the cheerful, teasing, kind man from the ball?

When Miss Darby's house came into view, Mr. Claridge took his leave, not pausing to bid her farewell. Amelia bit back her annoyance, plowing toward the front doors with Aunt Margaret beside her. She cleared her heart of any remaining unrest before knocking thrice on the smooth wood of the door.

"What do you think you are you doing?" Aunt Margaret asked.

Amelia's eyes widened as she stared at her fist that had just knocked against the door. She gasped. She was supposed to be awaiting Miss Darby and Miss Reed when they would leave for their walk. She could not simply knock on the door and invite herself in to meet Miss Darby when they had never met. Amelia froze as heavy footfalls reached her ears from behind the door. She had forgotten their plan! Mr. Claridge's strange disposition had muddled her mind.

Without thinking, she clutched Aunt Margaret's arm, pulling her down the steps and into the bushes that flanked the front path. Aunt Margaret hobbled into the bushes behind Amelia, muttering a phrase or two that could not be repeated.

Amelia put a finger to her lips, signaling her aunt to be silent. They waited, and Amelia listened to her heart pumping in her ears. The hinges of the door creaked open, rested in silence, then creaked closed. The door clicked shut.

Breathing out a sigh of relief, Amelia motioned for Aunt Margaret to follow her out the other side of the bushes. She stifled a laugh at the sight of her aunt's hair, tangled up in the leaves of the bush.

"If I did not love you so dearly, I might strike you with my cane," she grumbled.

They stepped—or rather stumbled—out of the bushes. Amelia smoothed out her own hair, for it had been tangled as well. "Why did you allow me to approach the front door? I was not thinking clearly." Amelia frowned.

Aunt Margaret merely shrugged, fishing a large leaf from her curls. Amelia's heart leapt as she heard the front door open again. A high, ringing voice wafted through the air like perfume, reaching down to the bushes where they stood, only partially concealed.

The voice stopped abruptly.

Amelia peered out from behind the bush, attempting to remain hidden. But her eyes locked with a young woman, likely near her same age.

"Good morning," Amelia said in a quick voice. She pulled Aunt Margaret out of the bush and into view, straightening her own posture and offering a smile. Any intention she had about looking presentable and trustworthy were now vain pursuits. Amelia cringed at how she and Aunt Margaret must have appeared, emerging from the bushes in such a shocking manner. In fact, she couldn't imagine that emerging from bushes could be performed in a way that would not be shocking.

"What are you doing in our bushes?" The young woman asked, scrunching her brow. She wore a pale pink gown trimmed with intricate lace points. Her blonde hair was pulled back tightly with two small curls framing her sharp eyes.

"Oh!" Amelia searched her mind for a plausible excuse. "Yes, my apologies for the intrusion. My aunt has . . . lost her cat, and I fear the animal has wandered into the foliage of your property. We thought we saw him hiding in this bush." Amelia patted the plant awkwardly.

"I must find him or my heart shall burst with grief." Aunt Margaret covered her face with her hands, offering a display of pretend weeping that made Amelia cringe yet again.

"How impolite of me," she said. "Allow me to make my introduction. I am Miss Amelia Buxton, and this is my aunt, Miss Margaret Buxton."

Half expecting to be snubbed, Amelia was surprised to see compassion blooming on the young woman's face. She rushed down the steps to where they stood, bending over to peer into the bushes. "My name is Miss Darby," she said absentmindedly. "How dreadful that you have lost your cat! I would never have a dry eye for the remainder of my life should my cat disappear." She knelt on the ground, pursing her lips and offering a shockingly accurate *meow*. She glanced up. "He may come if he thinks I am a cat."

Amelia exchanged a look of dismay with Aunt Margaret.

"Quickly! Do exactly as I, for he will be bound to come if there is more than one cat." Miss Darby gestured for them to join her on the ground.

Aunt Margaret shook her head in mock regret. "I cannot, for I am stricken with a bad leg. But my niece will be quite glad to join you."

Amelia narrowed her eyes for only her aunt to see, crouching down by the bush. She peered into the dark tangle of branches, leaves, and dirt. "Come now, cat. Come out."

"You must make the sounds," Miss Darby snapped. "Like this: *Meowwww.*"

Amelia offered her best representation of a cat as Aunt Margaret shook with silent laughter from above. The bush did not stir. Amelia felt positively ridiculous calling for an imaginary cat. She found it odd that Miss Darby would take such great lengths to find a missing cat and yet sit in her drawing room with a piece of embroidery while she had a missing friend.

"What is his name?" Miss Darby said in an urgent voice.

"His name?"

Miss Darby lay on her stomach in the grass, shaking the bush with one hand. She raised her eyebrows. "Yes, his name."

"Adam," Amelia blurted the first name that came to her mind.

Miss Darby scowled. "How peculiar. I would never think to give my cat such a boring name."

"Nor would I," Amelia said. "But it is not my cat. My aunt has rather boring taste, I must confess."

"I see." Miss Darby glanced up at Aunt Margaret, who cast Amelia a scowl before forcing the end of her cane into the small of Amelia's back.

"Ow!" Amelia called out, rolling to her side.

"That is wrong," Miss Darby corrected in a haughty voice. "It is *meow.*"

When Miss Darby had finally determined that the ficti-tious cat would never be found, she brushed off her dress, standing with a look of despair. "My sincere condolences to you both. I cannot comprehend how distraught you must feel." She blinked her large eyes rapidly, as if moved to emotion, pressing her hand to her chest. "Please, ac-company me on my morning walk. Perhaps we will find your cat along our way."

Amelia smiled. "Thank you. Your kindness is too much."

"Yes, I have been told such before." Miss Darby ex-tended her arm to Amelia. "My friends regard me as their kindest acquaintance." She extended her other arm to Aunt Margaret with a warm smile.

"Do you have many friends here in Brighton?" Amelia asked as they walked, sensing an opportunity to bring Eleanor into the conversation.

"Not many, but a few that are very dear to me." Miss Darby stared straight ahead. Amelia struggled to keep up with her pace. She could only imagine how Aunt Marga-ret must have felt, limping along on the other side of their new friend.

Amelia studied Miss Darby's profile. "How wonderful it is to have dear friends."

"It is wonderful indeed. Dear friends are difficult to find. Trustworthy, kind, agreeable
people to befriend even more so."

"I agree. Perhaps you might tell me who these friends of yours are, so I may have a place to begin. I have very few friends here in Brighton."

Amelia waited for Miss Darby's reply, keeping her ex-pression free of suspicion.

"Yes, of course. I have two friends that I treasure most.

Miss Reed and Miss Claridge." Expecting Miss Darby to clarify that Miss Claridge was currently missing, Amelia was surprised when Miss Darby's words stopped there.

"Where might I find these lovely ladies? I hope to have a small garden party before the season's end, and I should like only the most amiable of people in attendance."

Miss Darby's eyes flickered to Amelia's before turning swiftly back to the road ahead. They passed closer to the ocean, a breeze picking up and twisting Miss Darby's curls about her forehead. "Miss Reed lives just up the road. You will have the privilege of meeting her soon. She will take our walk with us. I shall introduce you."

"And the other friend?"

"Who?"

"The one you called Miss Claridge, if I recall." Amelia watched Miss Darby's jaw tighten in small increments. Her throat bobbed with a swallow.

"Oh, yes. Miss Claridge—well, she has not been seen for some time now. I haven't the slightest idea of where she is." Miss Darby's voice came out quick. "Oh, there is Miss Reed!"

A young lady with auburn hair waved from the door of a small house in the distance. She rushed down the steps, intercepting the trio as they walked past on the cobble-stone path. As Miss Reed came closer, Amelia could see the abundance of freckles on her face, and the inviting smile that she cast to both Amelia and Aunt Margaret.

Amelia forced herself to return the smile, eager to continue the conversation with Miss Darby. Eleanor's name had already been spoken in their conversation. If Amelia raised more questions later Miss Darby might grow suspicious.

After their introductions had been made to Miss Reed,

the group carried on in their walk each woman taking her own pace. Amelia lengthened her stride, keeping pace with Miss Darby. "I am sorry our conversation was interrupted. Do I recall hearing you say that your dearest friend Miss Claridge is missing? How dreadful!"

A twinge of annoyance twisted Miss Darby's delicate features before they became smooth once again. Just as Adam had described, there was no sign of distress on her face. "Yes. I have been unable to eat or sleep for days. The fresh seaside air is the only remedy I have found for my nerves. I do hope she is found soon."

"We must conduct our own search for her! Surely you know her character better than most. You may be able to provide necessary details that might lead to her discovery."

Miss Darby opened her mouth to speak but closed it again, stumbling over her words. "Why, yes, what a clever idea, Miss Buxton. I—I shall consider it."

"Have you any idea of where she may be located?" Amelia asked. She felt close to discovering something. A clue that might give her and Adam direction in their search.

"Not the slightest. I told you before. But I wish I did." Miss Darby's words were final, and she looked straight into Amelia's eyes.

"Do you think she is alive?" Amelia said in a hushed voice.

Miss Darby jerked her head in Amelia's direction, and for the first time, Amelia saw a hint of worry behind her eyes. "Yes. She must be alive. I cannot countenance the idea that she is not. Never speak of it again."

Amelia held her gaze, searching for hints there. But Miss Darby's eyes were like the ocean beside them, blue and simple on the surface, but hiding things beneath that one could only imagine.

Amelia tried to hide her disappointment. Today was not the day she would coerce the information out of Miss Darby that she sought. Ironically, Miss Darby seemed to value trust above all else. Amelia would have to win her trust before she would reveal anything to her.

As they walked, Amelia took the opportunity to ask Miss Darby more about herself and her family. If nothing else, the woman enjoyed speaking of herself. She went on for several minutes about her cats, her sisters, and finally her parents. Amelia listened with only half an ear, using what remained of her attention to puzzle through what she had just seen and heard. Miss Darby claimed to have no knowledge of Eleanor's location, or to be distressed by her disappearance, yet she had seemed reluctant to even tell Amelia that her friend was missing. She had clearly shown her discomfort with the topic, and had put an end to it.

"Are there any men in town that you fancy?" Miss Darby's voice crashed back into Amelia's ears.

"Oh, I have had little time to socialize," Amelia stammered.

"The men in Brighton have only become more plentiful in recent years," Miss Reed added. "Why should I desire a season in London when so many eligible men travel to Brighton?"

"There is only one man I desire," Miss Darby said in a wistful voice. "I am quite certain I will never find another man to be so handsome and agreeable."

Miss Reed spun with a giggle, holding her bonnet atop her head as the wind whipped her hair. "Lord Ramsbury is all she ever speaks about."

"He is the most wonderful man that has ever graced my presence." She sighed, spinning to face Amelia more fully. "If I cannot marry him I will tear my eyes out, for

I will be so depressed I shall never see the world in color again."

Amelia stopped her shock from showing. Miss Darby's extreme attachment to Lord Ramsbury could prove problematic to their friendship.

How could she court Lord Ramsbury and build a friendship with Miss Darby in the process? Miss Darby would likely tear *Amelia's* eyes out if she learned of her betrayal, courting the man she had already claimed.

It seemed there would be no limits to Amelia's deception.

"I have never met this Lord Ramsbury," she said.

"Oh, you will scarcely be able to keep your wits about you if you do. There is no man equal in charm or grace. Or wealth for that matter. He is the eldest son of the earl of Coventry. He is likely soon to die and Lord Ramsbury shall then inherit the title and estate." Miss Darby gave a wicked smile. "Lady Coventry. Does that not sound divine?"

"Indeed, it does." Amelia could not believe her lack of luck. Why could Miss Darby not be enamored with a different man? This town was home to hundreds, even thousands. How Lord Ramsbury's charm captivated so many women could not be explained.

As they finished their walk, Miss Darby waved in farewell. "I do hope you find your cat, Miss Buxton. I shall keep my eyes open."

Aunt Margaret pressed her hand to her heart. "Thank you, my dear. I miss my Adam dearly."

Amelia fought her smile as they turned around and began their walk back to the beach where the real Adam awaited them. Aunt Margaret limped, a look of concealed pain in her turquoise eyes. She hid it with a smile. "I cannot wait to see Mr. Claridge's reaction when he learns you named a pretend cat after him." She released a hoot of laughter.

"No! You must not tell him that!"

"Why ever not?" Aunt Margaret asked with a twinkle of mischief. "I daresay he will be flattered that you think so fondly of him."

Amelia rolled her eyes. "Fondly enough to give an imaginary cat his name."

"His Christian name, no less."

Amelia squeezed her eyes shut. She could not have Mr. Claridge discovering such an embarrassing thing.

"Oh, not to worry, child. I shall leave you to meet with him alone. I must return home and rest." She bit her lower lip, cringing in pain.

"Do you need help?" Amelia asked, holding her aunt by the arm.

"Not at all. Go on." Aunt Margaret nodded toward where the path split. "You may be in the sole company of Mr. Claridge all afternoon if you wish, or should I say . . . the company of *Adam*." Another devious smile pulled on her lips. Before Amelia could question what it meant, her aunt walked away down the path leading to their house, leaving Amelia to face Mr. Claridge alone.

Chapter 10

$\mathcal{A}$melia froze in her place, considering following her aunt home and not meeting Mr. Claridge at all. He had treated her with such disdain this morning. He had acted as if they were not even friends. Were they friends? She thought of him as a friend, but it was true that she did not have many friends. Perhaps she didn't fully understand the meaning, even after receiving Miss Darby's thorough and hypocritical explanation of the meaning of friendship.

But Amelia was sure that the version of Adam she had seen that morning was not the sort of man she wished to have as a friend. He had been stern and cold. Would he be the same now? Her stomach twisted with dread upon the thought of seeing him again. It had hurt more than she cared to admit to be snubbed by him. Why did she care so much?

With a deep breath, she started toward the right side of the fork, coming closer and closer to their meeting place on the beach. If Mr. Claridge planned to snub her, she would just snub him in return. In the distance, Amelia saw him, his back toward her at the shoreline. A few small groups of people passed between them, parasols and fans in hand, scattered along the beach like colorful shells. Mr. Claridge stood, tossing stones into the waves again, periodically searching the sand for new ones.

She stopped at the top of the bank, watching as he tossed a large stone into the water, his sleeves rolled up to his elbows. Her heart skipped and she scolded it for doing so. Why did he affect her so severely? It was perfectly natural to be attracted to a handsome man, she reminded herself. It was nothing more than that. Gathering her courage, she walked closer to him from behind, her feet making no sound as they touched the sand.

Mr. Claridge glanced over his shoulder, as if he had sensed her there. He tilted his head, squinting against the sun, his eyes meeting hers. He lifted a hand in greeting. Amelia felt her knees wobble a bit when his mouth lifted in a tentative smile.

Something fierce and defensive rose up inside her. Now he cared to see her, but was it only because she might have information that he wanted? Was that all she meant to him? Was she simply a vessel of information to him?

With determination in her steps, she walked down the sand toward him. "Have my eyes deceived me, or did you actually acknowledge my presence?"

A deep crease marked his forehead. "What do you mean?"

She planted her hands on her hips. "This morning you acted as if I had ceased to exist. Do not deny it. And I have figured out why you acted in such a way."

His face seemed to lose a bit of color, his brows drawing together. He kicked the sand around his feet, avoiding her eyes once again. "Have you? Please enlighten me."

"You only wish to be near me when I have information about your sister. I am nothing more than a—than a... book. I am nothing more than a book to you. A vessel for information that you simply toss aside when you are finished with it."

Adam's eyes flew up to hers, amusement shining within them. He looked to be on the brink of laughter. Amelia couldn't believe it. He would dare laugh at her? Much to her dismay, he threw his head back in a deep laugh. "You are not a book, Amelia."

She stared at him. Had he just used her Christian name? He seemed to recognize his folly, pressing his lips together. "Miss Buxton."

In truth, he had been simply Adam in her mind since the night they had danced at the ball. To know that her Christian name came naturally upon his lips warmed her to her toes.

"You cannot reclaim your words once they have been spoken," she said. "Much like you cannot reclaim your actions. I thought you hated me this morning." Amelia was surprised by the hurt she felt welling up in her chest.

"Are you suggesting that I call you Amelia from now on?"

"Perhaps, we are soon to be engaged after all. But I am also suggesting that you apologize."

He chuckled. "I am sincerely sorry, Amelia." The emphasis he placed on her name made a smile pull at her lips. The ways of Brighton were different from the ways of the rest of the country. Social propriety didn't seem as important as it had in Nottingham. She found she quite liked it. "I do not know what came over me," Adam said. "I suppose I forgot that a woman expects to be treated in a certain fashion by her intended."

Amelia looked away from his eyes. They were much too blue and staring far too intently into hers.

She released a quiet laugh. "All I ask is that I not be treated like a book."

"That is truly all you ask?

Amelia thought for a moment before answering. "Yes. That is all."

He shrugged, tossing his hands in the air. "If you are certain." His face held every sign of a tease, and Amelia couldn't help but press further.

"What else might I ask for?"

He exhaled slowly, bending over and sitting on the sand, tracing circles in it with his finger, facing the ocean. Amelia pressed her knees together, taking a place beside him, covering her feet with her skirts. The nearby ocean filled the air with the music of nature— the crashing of waves a symphony, and the gentle breeze a chorus.

Adam tossed a small pebble into the water. "You might ask that I treat you as if you truly were engaged to me."

Amelia laughed. "But I am not."

"Yes, but if you were, you would be a fortunate woman indeed."

She ignored the way her heart skipped as he leaned back on his hand, bringing himself closer to her.

Amelia rolled her eyes. "You claim that Lord Ramsbury is arrogant. You might consider listening to yourself speak."

His mouth split into a smile, and she noted the creases that formed at the corners of his eyes. She had never noticed them before.

"As a child, I took notice of the manner in which my father treated my mother. She was his entire world. He adored her. I determined then that when the time came that I would marry, my wife would receive no less."

Amelia looked down to where his hand rested in the sand, an inch from her own. She swallowed against the dryness in her throat. She could smell him—the masculine and refreshing scent that she could only associate with seaside breezes and sunshine.

"I decided I would spend every moment of my life in pursuit of her happiness, because she would be the most prominent source of mine. I would listen to her, hold her hand when she was afraid, laugh with her over the simplest of things. I would give her everything she desired, and do everything in my capacity to take away the things that burdened her. To phrase it simply, I would love her."

Amelia thought of the woman that Adam would someday marry. A surge of jealousy gripped her heart. She pushed it away. The purpose of their arrangement was that she would never have to marry. Their engagement would be only be a ruse, a way for Amelia to escape a life tied to managing a home and children and eventually growing resentful of the person who took her freedom. Amelia refused to one day be looked at the way she had seen her father look at her mother.

"I am not going to ask that you love me, Mr. Claridge," Amelia said. She willed her voice not to shake. She smiled up at him, hoping to lighten the tension she felt by his closeness.

His gaze clung to her face a brief moment longer before he tossed another pebble into the water. "Yes, because you do not believe in love."

"I cannot believe in something that I have not seen.

Perhaps love exists, but it is fickle. It may appear to be lasting and real, but eventually it fades and dies."

"Do you consider love to be an irrational idea?" he asked, picking up a handful of sand.

"Yes, precisely."

Adam smiled as if he had just found a trunk of gold in the sand beneath them. "I recall being told that intelligence requires an open mind—to see the irrational thought to carry as much possibility as the rational."

Amelia glanced at him from the corner of her eye. He had caught her in a contradiction. But love was different. He had quoted her from the moment she had been defending the cure of the Brighton waters. That was just a silly thing. Love was a rather serious one.

"Love is irrational," she repeated.

"But not impossible."

She dared a look at his eyes and wished she hadn't. Her heart fluttered around in her chest, its wings spreading farther and farther, brushing against the walls she had surrounded it with. She caged it in, refusing to believe Adam's words or the things her heart wanted her to feel.

Brushing the sand from her lap, she stood, unable to sit near him a moment longer. She needed to clear her mind, and that most certainly would not happen with Adam only inches away.

"You should know," she said in a prim voice, "that I haven't yet any information from Miss Darby that you don't already possess. I did find her rather suspicious, and I will continue working to gain her trust. I know she is hiding something."

Adam hesitated on the ground, a deep crease marking his forehead. He moved to stand beside her. "I trust that you will discover the truth soon."

"I hope you are right. I fear Miss Darby may refuse to speak to me if she learns I am seeking after Lord Ramsbury."

"Why is that?"

"She is rather besotted with him." Amelia frowned. "Obsessively so."

He rolled his eyes, shaking his head. "Why is it that every woman in all of Brighton is besotted with him?"

"He *is* charming." Where credit was due, Lord Ramsbury could rob any woman of her wits with a simple smile.

"You find him charming?" Adam crossed his arms, raising his eyebrows in disbelief.

"Somewhat." It was a lie, of course, but Amelia was curious to see Adam's reaction.

His jaw tightened and he looked down at the sand at his feet. She hid her smile, a warmth threading over her entire body, reaching out to her fingertips. Could he be jealous?

"I am not in earnest," she said, her laughter muffled behind her hand.

He looked up from the ground, narrowing his eyes at her before his lips twisted into an unenthusiastic smile.

She sighed. "But if I hope to avoid any contention between Miss Darby and myself, I must keep my interactions with Lord Ramsbury far from the public. She mustn't see us together. I haven't any idea of how to accomplish that." She chewed her lip in thought.

"We will think of something," Adam said. He extended his arm to her. "I will walk you to your home. With both our minds at the task we are sure to find a solution."

Amelia took his arm, trying not to notice the lean muscle that lay beneath his sleeve.

The walk to her home was short, and their conversation did not bring about the hoped for solution. Amelia walked up the steps of the small townhouse, turning at the door to face Adam. "Would you like to come in? My aunt would enjoy your company." She smiled at him.

Adam's disposition shifted, his mouth returning to the firm line she had seen this morning. "I will take my leave, but thank you. I will call upon you tomorrow."

Amelia studied him in confusion as he walked down the steps and onto the road once again. How strange. She scowled at his back. She might have been imagining the coldness in his farewell, but she couldn't be certain. It was as if he were putting forth significant effort to keep himself distanced from her, but had slipped in his act at the beach.

Shaking away her troubled thoughts, she entered the house. She was surprised to find two red roses resting on the dining table. With a frown she walked toward them, setting her bonnet down beside them on the table. A small note was attached to one thorn covered stem.

Dearest Miss Buxton,

Each moment I have spent with you has claimed yet another piece of my heart. Let these roses represent my affection as you hold them near. I would be honored if you would agree to take a picnic with me at the beach near my home. I will arrive on the morrow at noon to convey us there.

With sincerity,

Lord Ramsbury

114

Amelia dropped the note on the table in alarm before picking it up again and gathering the roses in her hand. She needed to tell Adam at once.

Rushing back to the door, she ran down the steps. She could still see him, far in the distance.

"Mr. Claridge!" she shouted. Lifting her skirts, she raced across the stony path, careful not to slip on the sand that spilled under the soles of her boots.

"Mr. Claridge!"

He turned around fast. She waved the note and flowers in the air as she approached. Her steps slowed and she stopped in front of him, pushing the wild strands of hair from her eyes. "Tomorrow at noon," she said, breathless. "Lord Ramsbury is taking me on a picnic. It seems he intends to begin a true courtship with me." Panic clutched her stomach.

Adam glanced at the note in her hand, his features firm. "Perfect. As I promised, I will be there to ensure your safety."

"You musn't be seen," she reminded him.

He glanced up from the note, and for a moment his eyes brushed over her face. "With you nearby he will be incapable of noticing anything else. That I am certain of." Though his eyes were serious, a whisper of a smile touched his lips.

She looked down, cursing the blush at her cheeks. Had Adam just offered her a compliment? She couldn't be sure. She had grown far too used to Lord Ramsbury's blatant compliments, so she struggled to recognize a subtle and sweet one. But the effect it had on her was much different, a slow and quiet warmth spreading over her entire body, wrapping a blanket around her heart.

"I will follow from a distance on horseback," Adam said. "I will not be seen."

Amelia sniffed the roses in an effort to hide the awkwardness she felt at Adam's compliment. She laughed softly. "You may find it odd, but I have always been rather averse to roses. I do not enjoy the scent, and the flower itself is very dull, all wrapped up in a bud with no center to be seen. The thorns are bothersome as well." She sniffed them again before holding them at her side. "But I do appreciate the gesture, I suppose. Each one represents a piece of Lord Ramsbury's heart, you know."

Adam choked on a laugh, quickly turning it into a cough. "How thoughtful of him. But he might have asked what flower you prefered."

"At the very least." Amelia rolled her eyes teasingly.

"What is your favorite flower?"

"A lily. It was my mother's favorite flower. She often wore one in her hair, tucked in a ribbon at the back of her head." Her heart ached with longing for those childhood memories. She missed her mother fiercely. Her home had never been the same since the time her mother grew ill and passed away when Amelia had only been fifteen years old.

Adam gave a soft smile, a gentleness in his eyes that tugged at her emotions, threatening to untether them. "The things we love are often tied to the people we love."

"Yes," she whispered, her throat tight.

"I will see you tomorrow," Adam said, breaking the silence, "during your picnic with Lord Ramsbury."

"And I will *not* see you tomorrow, for you will be hidden."

"Precisely."

Amelia's stomach twisted into knots as she took her short walk back home. Tomorrow would be an eventful day indeed.

Adam pushed back the discontent that roiled in his chest as he made his way back to his house with hurried steps. He had promised his father a game of chess and he couldn't be late or he would risk being declared 'afraid' to play against his father.

He felt as though everything in his life were being held captive, trapped behind an iron door, halting all progression. He had little lead in his search for Eleanor and Amelia's stubborn mind could never be changed. He was drawn to her, and in their time together he suspected that she felt the same toward him. But her circumstances had led her to believe that love could never exist—that all a marriage could bring to her was suffering.

He had determined that morning before meeting with her that he would work to distance his heart from her. It would do him more harm than good to hear her laugh and see her smile and know he couldn't see it forever. But he had learned today that his heart was never safe with Amelia nearby, no matter how hard he tried. She had softened his facade with one look.

If only he could change her mind. But the effort was futile and it exhausted him. He had other matters that required his focus.

He checked his pocket watch. He had wasted an hour distracted by Amelia. He could have been studying, searching, furthering his efforts to find his sister. Guilt clawed at him once again.

As he looked up from his watch, he spotted two women rounding the path in front of him, stopping no less than ten feet away. Adam recognized them to be Miss Darby and Miss Reed. Miss Darby's eyes rounded and she tugged on the sleeve of her friend. Adam lengthened his stride toward them, offering a curt wave. The women could not escape him without passing directly by. His muscles tensed with anticipation. Here was an opportunity to speak to both Miss Darby and Miss Reed together.

He greeted them, hoping his face reflected gentleness. His harsh demeanor had not served him well the last time. "I'm afraid I have met little success in my search for Eleanor," he said.

Miss Reed shared a quick glance with her companion. Adam studied her expression—the guilt that hovered there. So it was not only Miss Darby that knew a piece of the truth.

Miss Reed shifted in her place, avoiding Adam's eyes. "Oh, dear. That is dreadful."

"Is it dreadful?" he asked, taking one pace forward.

Her green eyes flicked to his in shock. "Pardon me?"

"If there is anything you know about Eleanor that has been kept from me, I would ask that you reveal it to me at once. I must find Eleanor and bring her home."

Miss Reed scowled, her lightly visible brows drawing together. "Has it ever occurred to you that she may not wish to come home?"

Adam froze, his pulse echoing in his ears along with her words. Miss Darby thrust her elbow into Miss Reed's side, causing her to cringe.

Miss Reed touched her hair, attempting to appear nonchalant. "What I mean to say is—perhaps Eleanor is content where she is, wherever that may be. If I wish to live in peace I must force myself to have hope for her safe return."

Adam gathered his thoughts, mind spinning. "Do you

know where she is?" His voice came out louder than he intended.

She looked down at the ground. "I'm afraid not."

"Good day, Mr. Claridge, but we must take our leave. Miss Reed's complexion does not take well to excessive sunlight." Miss Darby threw him a warning with her eyes before pulling Miss Reed along in the opposite direction.

Adam's thoughts moved so quickly he struggled to grasp onto one long enough to make sense of it. *Has it ever occurred to you that she may not wish to come home?* No. It had never occurred to him. A great stone of dread seemed to settle in his chest. Where could she be? Could Eleanor's disappearance be intentional? He refused to believe it. Miss Darby and Miss Reed could still be deceiving him. They might have been trying to mislead him. And then there was Ramsbury. Adam hoped that Amelia could pull some truth out of him at their picnic tomorrow. Only time would tell.

Chapter 11

The next morning, Amelia was shocked to see a bundle of lilies resting on the table. She snatched them up, searching for a note, but found none. She did not need a note to know they came from Mr. Claridge. Her heart skipped as she brought the flowers to her nose, inhaling their sweet scent. How kind of him. Her eyes stung with tears as the tenderness of the gesture gripped her heart. The scent of the flowers reminded her of her mother.

Her eyes caught on another bouquet of roses on the opposite end of the table. Setting the lilies down gently where she had found them, she snatched the note from beside the roses, scanning her eyes over the page. She dropped it on the table.

It was signed, in a flourishing hand, *Mr. Booth.* The man truly did exist.

Amelia covered her mouth, letting out a sound of gleeful surprise. She rushed to Aunt Margaret's bedchamber where she had settled on her bed with a book. She had been awake for hours, and had surely seen the flowers already.

Aunt Margaret raised her eyes when Amelia entered, her round cheeks shaking with a girlish giggle. She knew what Amelia had seen.

"You are the most sought-after woman in all of Brighton!" Amelia sat on the edge of her aunt's bed, unable to contain her grin. "Mr. Booth hopes to court you, I think."

"I said as much." Aunt Margaret exercised great effort to keep her smile at a reasonable size, but her quivering cheeks showed that the exertion would be too much. She sat forward, her bright blue eyes rounding. "But do you really suppose he will?"

"It appears so!"

"Lord Ramsbury hopes to court you as well. It seems his feelings are genuine. He cannot be taking such steps toward *every* woman. He has shown an attachment to you, Amelia."

Her aunt's words brought Amelia's elation to an abrupt halt. Though vexing, Amelia couldn't countenance breaking Lord Ramsbury's heart. She hoped for his sake that he didn't care for her in the way Aunt Margaret implied. She certainly hoped he didn't intend to marry her. She swallowed her fear. How could she deceive him so?

"When shall I meet this Mr. Booth?" Amelia asked, pushing aside her fearful thoughts. "I should like to ensure he is worthy of my dearest aunt's heart."

Aunt Margaret chuckled. "There is not much to be worthy of, my dear. I am just a plain woman with a crippled leg."

"Oh, stop! You are far more than that! You are lovely in every way. You are kind, humorous, and one can never experience a dull moment with you."

Aunt Margaret looked down, a shyness about her that Amelia had never seen. "I never thought a man could be capable of overlooking my leg. I do not walk normally. I have never been graceful." She gave a quiet laugh, a seriousness claiming her countenance. "My first season in London years ago taught me that a man looks only on the surface of a woman. On her beauty, on those things that made her desirable. I suppose I gave up on men long ago, when one man tossed me aside in London because I was not pretty enough."

Amelia listened in silence, her eyes burning with emotion. She had not known this story of Aunt Margaret's past. Amelia had never considered the emotional struggle Aunt Margaret must have faced with her leg. She had assumed she only wanted it healed to avoid discomfort.

"I did not think it possible for a man to overlook my flaws of appearance," Aunt Margaret continued, "but Mr. Booth has."

Amelia smiled, but her mind burned with suspicion of this man. How could love begin to form so quickly? She could not judge his character without meeting him, but if he ventured to break her aunt's heart, Amelia would see to it that he regretted it. She wanted to believe in love. Seeing her aunt, a woman whom she had always admired, and a woman who had even greater reason to doubt love, with the sparkle of love now shining in her eyes, gave Amelia a new kind of hope. She struggled to make sense of it as she reached for her aunt's hand.

"Perhaps you do not need the waters to cure your leg," Amelia said. "Your beauty extends beyond that."

"Oh, I still hope they will cure me. I plan to dip again on the morrow. Will you join me?"

"No, thank you." Amelia offered in a quick voice, standing from the bed.

"Yes! You must. I insist."

Amelia had nearly escaped to the doorway. She squeezed her eyes shut. Drat. How could she refuse? "Very well. But you mustn't trick me again! I was convinced that I would be dipping unclothed."

Aunt Margaret tossed her head back in laughter, her blonde curls bouncing on her shoulders.

Two hours later, with Amelia dressed in her favorite lavender gown, she moved to the front window, awaiting Lord Ramsbury's carriage. Her heart beat fast, causing her legs to shake with nervousness. Despite hardly knowing her, she felt as if she were betraying Miss Darby by spending the day with Lord Ramsbury. But she also felt as if she were betraying Adam. He was her fiancé after all. Her *pretend* fiancé, she reminded herself.

The longer she stood there at the window, she found herself wishing she was taking this picnic with Adam and not Lord Ramsbury. How much more relaxing and diverting it would be. She enjoyed talking with Adam. He did not press her to explain things that hurt to speak about. He listened and laughed. She thought of his smile and his lively blue eyes. She had not seen the heavy sorrow within them since the first time they met. She hoped she had helped dispel that sorrow in some way during their time together. Her heart gave a distinct leap at the thought of their conversation on the beach the day before, when he had spoken of his future wife. A part of her longed for the things he spoke of, but the other part, the greater part of her was afraid. She could not tell if her feelings were real or a ruse. After all, their engagement would only be a ruse.

She pressed her face against the cool glass of the window. She wished Aunt Margaret was still here, but she had left to meet Mr. Booth at the card room. It seemed Amelia could no longer rely on her aunt to support her argument against love.

As Amelia puzzled through the feelings in her heart, she decided that if love was indeed real, she felt a small part of it for Mr. Adam Claridge. The thought shook her, filling her mind with tendrils of doubt. She shunned her thoughts away as an extravagant phaeton came to a halt out the front window. She glanced at the clock. It read exactly twelve.

Lord Ramsbury stepped down from the high seat, landing gracefully on the ground, his tailcoat swaying. The Phaeton's wheels seemed to be nearly as tall as him, sturdy and bold. She stared at the horses that drew the phaeton, nervous at the realization that they would be their only chaperones. With a rush of relief she remembered that Adam would be there too, following secretly. She smiled, squinting out the window. Where could he be hiding? She felt very much like a spy on a secret quest. In truth, that was precisely what she was. Guilt gnawed unexpectedly at her stomach when she saw that Lord Ramsbury was in possession of another rose.

She opened the door to the townhouse, stepping out to meet him. His hair shone golden brown in the sunlight, and his deep set eyes bore into hers, the intense blue almost shocking. He wore a simple waistcoat and jacket, a much less foppish choice than he usually flaunted. She detected a sort of shyness in his smile as he looked down at her. He tore his eyes from her face, taking her hand in his and placing a kiss on top of it.

"You look enchanting, Miss Amelia. I expect my roses found you well?"

"Yes, they were lovely." Her heart sunk at the look of hope in Lord Ramsbury's eyes.

"You liked them?"

She struggled to keep his gaze. "Yes, of course. I thank you for that thoughtful token."

"That is very good." He gave one of his charming smiles, extending his arm to her. She was surprised at the way he was acting. He was still confident, but she could also sense a bit of nervousness in his movements. Lord Ramsbury nervous? She hadn't thought it possible.

"I hoped you wouldn't object to spending more time with me. I enjoy your company and conversation very much," he said as they walked to the phaeton. "My servants have prepared a feast for us." He watched for her reaction.

She smiled, willing herself to appear as excited as he hoped she would be. "I look forward to it. I am starved." She patted her middle before realizing how ridiculous she must have looked.

Lord Ramsbury laughed as he helped her into the tall seat of the phaeton. He climbed up beside her, making the entire contraption shift sharply with his weight. She screeched, accidentally gripping his hand for balance. She pulled her hand away as quickly as it came, but Lord Ramsbury took it back, stealing it from her lap. He bent his head, placing another kiss on the top of her hand before letting it go. She met his eyes, unsettled by the sincerity there.

"You may hold my hand at any moment, my dear." He traced her face with his gaze before gripping the reins and setting the horses at a slow pace. "Just not while I'm driving the phaeton." He shot her a teasing smile.

Amelia gave an awkward laugh, shifting her leg so it did not rest against his. Why must the seat be so small?

The ride took less than ten minutes, and Amelia passed the time battering Lord Ramsbury with question after question that were hardly related to Eleanor, but that might lead him to mention her. None of her tactics worked. By the time they arrived at the beach, Amelia had almost run out of ideas. As Lord Ramsbury helped her down from the phaeton, she stole a quick glance behind them. She could see no sign of Adam.

The beach, wide and expansive, allowed little place for Adam to watch and remain concealed. She knew his motive was not to overhear the conversation, but to rise to action should Lord Ramsbury turn out to be a threat to Amelia. But the more time she spent with Lord Ramsbury, Amelia realized she was more of a threat to him. She was stealing his heart with no intention of giving him hers. She tried to comfort herself, to justify her actions. Once she had gained the information she sought, she would convince him that his feelings for her were not real. How could they be? He was simply confused. She could convince him that she was only another of his many flirtations, nothing more.

"What do you think of this place, just here?" Lord Ramsbury walked toward a spot of dry sand, far enough from the ocean to avoid getting wet, but close enough to hear the natural music of the waves.

"That looks positively perfect." Amelia stood nearby, adjusting her bonnet as a gust of wind untethered it from her head.

Lord Ramsbury looked up from where he was spreading a quilt, dropping it on the ground. "Allow me." He walked toward her. Leaning his head down in focus, he grasped the ribbons of her bonnet and secured them under her chin. He gazed into her eyes, brushing a strand of loose hair away from her forehead. Amelia knew she was supposed to act as if she welcomed his attention, but her conscience would hardly allow it. Part of Amelia hoped that Lord Ramsbury was the culprit of Eleanor's disappearance. Only then might she justify the deceit she was putting Lord Ramsbury through.

She looked down as he dropped his hand from her face. Sweeping her lavender skirts beneath her, she sat down. Lord Ramsbury joined her after fetching a large basket from the phaeton. He opened it, withdrawing fanciful dishes and silver. After filling Amelia's plate with an assortment of breads, cheeses, meats, and fruit, he filled his own, speaking in raptures about his childhood picnics on the beach with his family.

"I am the eldest child, and also favored least of my parents." He chuckled. "My father claims that I need to marry soon."

"As does mine," Amelia said with a sigh. She pressed her lips together, immediately regretting her words.

Lord Ramsbury leaned back on his hand, bringing himself closer to her. "How fortuitous that we should both have fathers insisting upon our marriage." He threw her a wink. She swallowed. She did not enjoy jesting about marriage unless it was with Adam. With him she knew they were only jesting, but with Lord Ramsbury . . . she felt he was far from it.

"I can never marry until I know my dear friend Eleanor has returned home safely," Amelia said. "As children we promised one another that we would never miss the other's wedding. I could never break that promise." Amelia bit half off of a grape, trying to appear nonchalant while her heart raced in her chest. How would he reply?

His gaze faltered, just as it had the first time she had mentioned Eleanor's name. "Do you wonder . . . if perhaps Miss Claridge will not return?" Lord Ramsbury said after a long stretch of silence.

Amelia pressed her hand to her heart. "Why ever would you suggest such a thing? I refuse to believe I have lost her forever."

He pushed his food around his plate with a fork, feigning intense interest in the crust of his bread. "I am not suggesting that she is dead. I am simply opening your mind to the possibility that she may be lost, but perhaps lost of her own will and choice."

"What do you mean?" Amelia turned to face him more fully, the demure voice she had been flaunting disappearing. She was close—so close to learning his secret.

He set his jaw, keeping her gaze without a blink. After a long moment, he gave a soft shake of his head. "The secret is not mine to tell," he said. "But I will tell you this. I do not know where Miss Claridge is."

Amelia's heart pounded in her ears. "Are you suggesting that Eleanor simply ran away? Alone? Why would she do such a thing?"

Lord Ramsbury exhaled, long and slow, a certain frustration in his expression. "I made a promise to my friend as well. One that I mustn't break. I cannot give you further information about Miss Claridge. But you must believe that she will reveal herself in due time."

Amelia could scarcely believe what she was hearing. In her mind she had only considered the possibility that Eleanor had been abducted or worse. She had not considered that she might have chosen to disappear. Amelia did not know Eleanor herself, but she felt as if she knew her through Adam. Amelia couldn't claim to understand

Eleanor's character, but Lord Ramsbury's words did not feel true. Why would Eleanor desert her loving family?

Lord Ramsbury pulled another bunch of grapes from his basket. Amelia glared at him while he could not see her. She did not trust his words.

He turned toward her again and she smiled, taking a sip from her tea cup. "I thank you for being honest, my lord."

He gazed at her, the adoration in his eyes evident. He took the liberty to touch her arm. "I wish there was more I could say. But please trust that Eleanor is alive and will be heard from soon."

What did that mean? How did Lord Ramsbury know Eleanor was alive? Was he holding her captive? Was he an accomplice to one holding her captive? Amelia thought of the man of the regiment that Lord Ramsbury had been speaking to that first day at the assembly rooms. Their conversation had been hushed and their expressions had been fearful. Could that man be the guilty one?

Amelia decided to drop the subject for now, eager to tell Adam everything she had learned. She would need to continue building trust with Lord Ramsbury.

For the next hour their conversation turned to lighter things. They spoke of their families, favorite activities, poetry, music, and humorous stories from their childhoods. As they spoke, Amelia couldn't help but doubt that Lord Ramsbury could do anything so wicked. He seemed full of energy, light, and joy as he spoke, smiling without fail. Any false pretenses he had worn the first day they met had diminished now that they were away from the eye of the public. He gave the occasional compliment, and to Amelia's dismay she now found them to be much more genuine. Despite the fact that she still carried suspicion, her guilt rose with every word and every smile he gave her. She could practically see his heart in his eyes, not knowing that it would soon be shattered by her hand.

By three o'clock, it seemed that Lord Ramsbury would spend the entire day there if he could. Amelia knew it would be impossible to bring Eleanor into the conversation again, so she pretended she was feeling ill so he would take her home. Before she stepped inside, Lord Ramsbury took her hand in his. "May I see you at the assembly rooms tomorrow come noon? We might take a trip to the shops and explore the assembly rooms. I never did finish the tour I promised you."

Amelia nodded with effort. "There is nothing I would like more."

"Perfect!" Lord Ramsbury's enthusiasm had a boyish endearment that made Amelia feel truly ill. She was a terrible person, she decided as she closed the front door behind her. She was deceitful and cruel. She was toying with the man's heart in a despicable way. She didn't know how much longer she could carry on.

She watched as he drove the phaeton down the road until it was out of sight. She needed to find Adam. Tightening her bonnet, she sneaked out the front door, scanning the surrounding area. "Mr. Claridge?" she whispered.

She peered into the bushes near her door, the action feeling very reminiscent of the day she had searched the bushes at Miss Darby's home for an imaginary cat by the same name. She felt ridiculous. Adam would not be hiding in the bushes. He was not nearly as doltish as she was.

"Adam?" she called.

"I hope you never find your cat," a voice spat from behind her.

Amelia whirled around to see Miss Darby, eyes red and

burning with anger. Tears streamed down her cheeks. "I cannot blame Adam for running away. There is no cat that would like to be pet to such a liar."

Amelia recovered from her shock, stepping toward her. "Miss Darby, what is the matter?" She tried to reach for her hand, but Miss Darby slapped it away as if it were a large insect.

"You are courting Lord Ramsbury! You are courting my true love in secret! Never have I experienced such betrayal!" Miss Darby heaved a heavy sob, her hair sticking to her wet cheeks.

Amelia's eyes widened in shock. She stood there, unsure of what to do or say. Any expectation Amelia had of gaining Miss Darby's trust evaporated into the air between them.

"You acted as if you did not know Lord Ramsbury, when in reality you meant to steal him from me!" Miss Darby marched toward her, hands planted on her hips.

Taking a step back, Amelia held up her hands in defense. "I do not intend to marry Lord Ramsbury. I never have."

"That is the worst lie, but certainly not the only one, that has ever escaped your mouth." Miss Darby sniffed, her eyes narrowing. Amelia doubted she could even see her with such tears wobbling over her eyelids. "You hope to become Lady Coventry. I cannot allow any woman to steal that name from me. I am in love with him!"

"Yes, I see that," Amelia softened her voice, taking yet another step back as Miss Darby advanced toward her. She was beginning to think Miss Darby was insane. Amelia hoped Adam was nearby, perchance Miss Darby intended to harm her. The thought seemed absurd, but the rage glowing in Miss Darby's eyes could not be ignored.

"I will tell him that I no longer wish to see him. Then may we be friends again?"

Miss Darby scoffed. "Friendship cannot be born under such deceit and betrayal. I shall never forgive you for what you have done." She lifted her chin, slapping the tears from her cheeks before turning on her heel and stomping away down the path.

Amelia couldn't move. She stared at Miss Darby's retreating form, covering her mouth in astonishment. How could Miss Darby be so possessive of a man that she hardly knew?

A deep chuckle came from somewhere beside her. Amelia jerked her gaze to the right, where the real Adam—not the cat—came stepping out from behind the bush. He brushed a leaf from his hair, meeting her eyes with amusement.

"I knew you were hiding in the bush!" Amelia pointed an accusatory finger at him.

He grinned, stumbling over a loose branch in the dirt. He regained his footing with a laugh. "Miss Darby has never been a woman of a quiet disposition."

Amelia put her hand to her forehead. "I might be ill. I have betrayed her trust. She will never speak to me again."

"I may be mistaken, but did I hear Miss Darby mention a cat by my name?" Adam raised an eyebrow. "That may require an explanation."

Amelia's eyes flew open and her cheeks burned in embarrassment. "In order to gain her friendship the first time, I may have invented a ruse that I was searching for a cat on her family's property. Why I called him by your name I cannot explain."

Adam's smile was contagious, and Amelia couldn't help but laugh, in particular when she noticed the leaf that still clung to his dark hair. Without thinking, she rose on her toes and plucked it from the side of his head. She brushed his hair back into place, her fingers freezing there when her eyes shifted to his. The warmth in his gaze captivated her, setting her heart racing. Her height only brought her face to his cravat, but with his head tipped down to look at her, he was close enough to kiss. She shook herself. What was wrong with her?

She dropped her hand with a quiet laugh. "I hid myself in a bush that day as well."

"Did you?" His voice was soft, filled with quiet amusement.

"Indeed. I cannot claim to be proud of that decision."

He laughed again, and Amelia paused to admire the sound, wondering if she could ever grow tired of it. A pang of sadness overcame her at the realization that after their false engagement had been broken and her father fooled, Adam would leave and she would likely never see him again. Her heart ached at the thought.

"There is much I need to tell you," she said, searching for a distraction. "But first I must thank you for the lilies this morning."

Adam gave a shy smile. "You are quite welcome."

She searched his face, looking for answers there. Had he send the lilies to her because he cared for her? Or had he sent them as a simple gesture toward the loss of her mother? All she knew was that she would treasure those flowers more than a hundred roses from Lord Ramsbury.

Adam still stared at her, that endearing smile on his lips. Amelia cleared her throat, returning to the more important issue she wished to discuss.

"While Lord Ramsbury spoke little of Eleanor today, he did say something of great interest," she said.

Adam's face grew serious. "I have learned something as well. I passed Miss Darby on the street just yesterday. Shall we go to my house to discuss this further? My notes are there, and you may meet my father. He has been curious to meet you. I told him you had proved very helpful in our search for Eleanor."

"Very well. My aunt is gone, so I have little else scheduled. She is spending the day with a man that she met at the ball. She is quite smitten with him, and it seems he is smitten with her as well." Amelia took Adam's arm. "I have never seen her so very happy."

Half of Adam's mouth lifted in a smile as he glanced down at her. "Have you met him?"

"No, but I hope he is a good and honorable man. She claims he is." Amelia's heart soared as she remembered Aunt Margaret's girlish joy over Mr. Booth's note and his roses that morning. Finally, a man had seen Aunt Margaret for the joy that she was. If Aunt Margaret could come to believe in love and marriage, then perhaps Amelia could as well.

Before long, they arrived at Adam's home. Charming and quaint, Amelia admired the smooth copper stone and large windows. Inside, the home appeared larger than it had on the outside, designed with tall, domed ceilings and white walls. The clean marble floor showed signs of age, the footfalls of generations leaving memories embedded within it.

"You have a beautiful home," Amelia said. Her voice echoed in the tall entryway.

"It has been in the family for many generations." Adam motioned for her to follow him to the right, where a hall led to a small library. "Father?" Adam pulled the door open, leaning his head through it. "I have brought Miss Buxton to make your acquaintance."

Amelia stepped into view of the doorway. A tall and exceedingly thin man stood at a bookcase, a pile of books in his shaking arms. What remained of his gray hair lay in thin swirls atop his spotted head. His eyes were sharp and blue like Adam's, and she could see a likeness to Adam in the smile that he gave her.

"Miss Buxton. It is an honor to meet you." He coughed into his elbow. Adam moved into the room, taking the stack of books from his father's hand, setting them on the table for him.

Amelia's heart skipped with admiration over the love and care in Adam's expression. She wished she had such a relationship with her own father. She didn't even dare speak to her father if he did not invite her first to do so.

"My son tells me that you have been a vital advantage in the search for my daughter," Mr. Claridge said as his cough subsided. His eyes filled with tears. "My gratitude exceeds the limits of my expression." His voice was rasped and soft.

She didn't know what to say. The humble gratitude in Adam's father was enough to bring tears to her own eyes. She had hurt Miss Darby, and she would surely hurt Lord Ramsbury. But to know that she had taken part in easing this poor man's burden lifted a burden within herself. "I will not rest until she is found," Amelia said.

"Nor will I," Adam said in a firm voice. Amelia met his gaze across the table, sharing a little smile of determination and hope.

"And nor will I," Mr. Claridge said from his seat at the table, looking up between her and Adam with mirth in his features. "The grave will not take me until I know my daughter is safe."

Adam gave his father's shoulder a squeeze. "Miss Amelia is here to give us the information she has recently discovered." He took a seat beside his father and Amelia sat in the chair beside him.

Mr. Claridge quickly pushed away from the table, a look of mischief shining in his eyes. He masked it well behind a yawn. "I am far too tired to think clearly at the moment. Allow me to rest. I will leave the two of you to discuss alone."

Adam turned in his chair. "Are you unwell?"

"I am only tired, not to worry. I hope your discussion meets with success." Mr. Claridge wobbled on his feet, gripping the back of his chair for balance.

"I will help you to your room," Adam said, standing to take his father's arm. "I will return shortly," he said to Amelia.

She returned his smile, trying to hide the panic in her eyes. Sitting alone in a quiet room with Adam would do little to protect Amelia's heart against him. She chewed the nail of her index finger as Adam took his father out the door. What was she so afraid of? He made her feel things she didn't recognize, things that frightened her, but he also made her feel absurdly happy. She could not ignore that.

But she was only here to discuss Eleanor and what she had learned from Lord Ramsbury, that was all. Eleanor was the most important matter to attend to, not the trivial matters of her heart. She could sort through that later. Today she would remain stoic and keep her head in control of her heart. Surely Adam would do the same. He knew his role in her effort to obtain spinsterhood and freedom. The sting in her heart surprised her. Was that still the life she wanted? Yes? Yes.

Satisfied with her resolve, she sat back and awaited Adam's return.

136

Chapter 12

Adam helped his father situate himself comfortably in bed, pulling the covers up to his chin. "Are you certain you are well?" he asked.

"Are you certain *you* are well?" his father questioned, one thick eyebrow raised. The pillow nearly engulfed his head, leaving just his face peeking out of a plume of soft pillow. "I saw the manner in which you looked at Miss Buxton. I daresay you are smitten, my boy." He chuckled.

Adam's first instinct was to defend himself, but he relented. The time for receiving his father's advice was drawing to a close. And he desperately needed it. "Is it truly so obvious?"

"I have scarcely seen anything more obvious," his father said through another laugh. He erupted in a bout of coughing, his slight frame shaking.

Sitting on the bed, Adam waited until his father's cough subsided.

"Did you not realize my designs in leaving the two of you alone?"

Adam scowled. "You left us that we might discuss Eleanor and how we mean to find her."

"Never have I met a greater nodcock." His father pushed himself up to a sitting position, looking Adam squarely in the eyes. "If my suspicions are correct, she seems rather smitten with you as well. She is a wonderful young lady; you have chosen well. She is much more agreeable than that dreadful Mr. Quinton that Eleanor hoped to marry."

"Mr. Quinton?" Adam frowned. He had not heard of Mr. Quinton.

His father sighed. "Yes. But that was long ago. I never did approve of the man. But you," he pointed a finger at him, "are an honorable man deserving of a woman like Miss Buxton. What the devil are you waiting for?"

Adam was shocked by his father's speech. He didn't know how to respond. His father thought Amelia returned his feelings, but he must have been wrong. "She does not believe in love, nor does she believe in marriage."

His father sat forward in emphasis. "Make her believe." He pointed in the direction of the door. "I will not die knowing my son has such a troubled heart. Nor will I die knowing my son to be so cowardly."

Adam narrowed his eyes, ignoring the grief that stabbed him at the mention of his father's death. "You cannot play such a card against me, father."

He chuckled. "It is one of the few cards I have left in my hand. Have you declared your feelings for her?"

He sighed in exasperation. "No, but it is not that

simple." His father didn't know about the arrangement. Amelia had agreed to a false engagement with him for the sole purpose of avoiding marriage altogether. They were only meant to be pretending.

"Love is never simple, Adam. Nothing worthwhile is ever simple."

Not long ago Adam had resolved to keep his heart locked away from Amelia. It had not worked, but he had tried. How could he risk a rejection from her? It would break him. His focus needed to be on finding Eleanor, but to do so had led him to Amelia. He could not have any hope of finding Eleanor if he chose to avoid Amelia. He also had no hope of keeping his heart if he chose to be near her.

"What do you suggest I do?"

"Go back to the library. Give her a lesson in love." Adam's father grinned.

"A lesson in love?"

"She cannot know something to be real if she has not experienced or witnessed it, can she? Show her a bit of romance, flattery, chivalry."

Adam swallowed, rubbing the back of his neck. He glanced at his father. "How do you suggest I do that?"

"Kiss her."

Adam jerked his eyes to the doorway, worried that Amelia might have heard his father. He shook his head. "That is far outside my bounds."

His father shrugged, settling his head back down on the pillow. "I suppose you are a coward after all."

Gritting his teeth, Adam stood up. He was not a coward. His father laughed at him, pointing a heavy-knuckled finger at the door. Without another word, Adam exited the room, anxiety coursing through his veins. He did not *have to* do it simply because his father told him to. Kissing Amelia without any agreement between them would likely scare her away from him forever. But they were to be engaged . . . could that justify it? No.

The library door hovered in front of him, halfway closed. With a deep breath, he pushed it open. Amelia looked up from the book she had been reading. She pushed back a wisp of straight golden hair that had fallen over her eyes. *Her eyes.* Adam couldn't recall ever seeing a more beautiful set of brown eyes. They shone with life and joy, framed with dark lashes.

Realizing how long he had been staring at her, he cleared his throat and walked into the room, forcing his legs not to shake. *Blast it.* Perhaps he was a coward.

"Is your father well?" Her voice cut through the quiet air.

Adam crossed to the table, pausing to move his chair closer to her before sitting down. He turned his head to look at her face. "He needs rest, that is all. It has been difficult for him to rest of late with Eleanor gone. I think it has intensified his illness."

"He is a very amiable man." Amelia looked down at her book again. There was a shyness about her that Adam didn't recognize. Perhaps he had sat down too close to her. He almost moved his chair but remembered his father's candid invitation.

"I am glad you were able to meet him," Adam said.

"As am I. My motivation to find your sister has now increased ten-fold." She cast him a quick glance before looking away again, her cheeks taking on an endearing pink hue. He could smell a faint lavender perfume upon her, fitting with the color of her gown.

He smiled, leaning his elbows onto the table. "I am glad to hear it."

She refused to look at him, her expression firm and un-smiling. "Shall we discuss my meeting with Lord Ramsbury?"

Yes. That was the true reason they were here. Adam shrunk back in his chair. "Of course. What did Ramsbury have to say?"

During their picnic, Adam had been watching from behind the steep bank that led to the wide beach. He had only been able to see them from a distance, and had not enjoyed the experience. Watching Lord Ramsbury taking Amelia's hand, touching her face, her hair, sitting so near to her, had filled him with undeniable envy. If Amelia could remain unaffected by Lord Ramsbury's attempts at wooing her, how could she possibly be affected by his? As Philip Honeyfield had said, Lord Ramsbury had a way with women ordinary men would never understand.

Amelia inhaled deeply. "I must confess, I did not fore-see his words. I am not certain he is innocent, but he made a suggestion to the effect that Eleanor ran away of her own will. He claimed that she would be heard from soon, but that her location was not his secret to reveal."

He reached in his pocket, withdrawing a sheet of parchment that he had been using to track any clues. "Miss Reed suggested the same thing to me when I passed her and Miss Darby." He spread the parchment in front of Amelia, pointing at the place he had recorded it. She threw him a look of awe, pulling the parchment closer.

"Two accounts cannot be ignored," she whispered. "But it could very well be a ruse."

Adam's mind raced. What could have compelled Elea-nor to leave her home and family? She had seemed happy. Nothing had seemed to be amiss.

Amelia dropped the parchment, turning in her chair so swiftly Adam wondered if she would fall off. Her eyes wide, she gasped. "You saw Miss Darby today when she discovered that I was courting Lord Ramsbury. You saw her reaction, did you not?"

"I did."

"Did you find it to be at all extreme?"

Adam nodded with emphasis. "Very much so."

Amelia's voice shook. "And I am merely a brief acquaintance of hers. Do you wonder how she might react if one of her dearest friends attempted to steal Lord Ramsbury from her?"

Realization dawned on him, crawling over his skin with cold fingers. "Lord Ramsbury mentioned that Eleanor fancied him. Do you suppose …"

"Miss Darby discovered her friend's betrayal and thought to free herself of such competition?" Amelia's voice was soft and filled with foreboding.

Adam considered the idea, dread pouring through him. "But how then would Lord Ramsbury know of her location as he claimed to you?"

She sighed, putting a hand to her forehead, squeezing her eyes closed in thought. "I do not know." Her eyes peeked at him from beneath her hand. "I shall go find him this very moment. I will force him to tell me the truth. All of the truth." She pushed away from the table, standing up.

Adam panicked. He stopped her, reaching up and grasping her hand. She froze, looking down with a frown.

"How do you plan to 'force him' to tell you?" Adam asked. He couldn't hide his smile of amusement.

She sighed, reclaiming her seat beside him. "I will. . .hold him by the hair of his head while you throw him a facer or two." She laughed, shaking her head. "He will be so frightened he may finally be willing to speak."

Adam threw his head back in laughter. "That is your best idea yet."

"Although, I must confess, Lord Ramsbury is not the man I thought he was," she said. "There is more depth to his character than I originally observed. He claimed to have a friend that knew of Eleanor's location, but that he had promised that friend he would keep their secret. And he promised me that Eleanor was safe. The more I ponder his words, the more genuine I find them to be. I do not think he was lying. I only wish I could convince him to tell me everything."

Desperation cried out in Amelia's eyes. He remembered what his father had told him just minutes before. *Give her a lesson in love. Show her a bit of romance.* He swallowed hard, cowardice rising in his throat.

"You must convince him of your feelings," Adam said, his voice too quick. He tried to calm his heart as it leapt around in his chest. "Whether it is true or not, you must show him how you care for him. Only when he is sure of your loyalty may he reveal all he knows to you."

Her eyebrows tilted down. "If he is indeed innocent, he does not deserve to be so deceived. I cannot break his heart further. I will never marry, and he must know that. It isn't fair what I am doing to him." She stood up, crossing the room to the tall window beside a bookcase. Hiding her face from him, she remained silent.

Adam stood up, following her to the window, stopping two feet behind where she stood. The royal pavilion could be seen from their vantage point, the golden stone bright under the afternoon sun.

"Please turn around, Amelia."

She covered her face with her hands before complying.

"I am atrocious." Her voice came out muffled behind her hands.

Adam shook his head, but realized she couldn't see it. Gathering his fortitude, he drew closer to her, hooking one finger around hers, gently pulling her hand away from her face. There it was again, the tell-tale blush on her cheeks. Adam's heart jumped in his chest like an uncooperative horse as her eyes found his. She quickly looked down to where he still held her small hand in his.

"You are not atrocious." He forced his next words from his throat, afraid to speak them aloud. "You are lovely in every way."

She shook her head. "A lovely person does not practice deceit as I have. How can I continue to hurt Lord Ramsbury in such a way? How can I encourage a man to lose his heart to me with no intention of giving mine in return?"

He found irony in the fact that Amelia so hated deceiving Lord Ramsbury, but she had happily agreed to deceive her father by entering a false engagement with Adam. She so hated breaking Lord Ramsbury's heart, yet here she was, threatening to break Adam's heart with every word, every smile, every laugh.

"A man does not require encouragement to lose his heart to you," he said in a quiet voice.

Amelia's eyes flew up to his.

"If love is not real, as you claim, then Lord Ramsbury will recover quickly," Adam said. "If love is not real then he is simply pretending, just as you are."

"Well—"

Adam stopped her. "You contradict yourself."

Amelia closed her mouth, silencing her retort. He could see a hint of belief behind her eyes, but she hid it with a scowl. His heart hammered in his chest, but he willed himself to have the courage to speak. And to act.

Drawing closer, he placed one hand on the window behind her, just above her shoulder, tilting his face down only inches from hers. "If love is not real, then please explain why I cannot keep my wits around you. Please explain why I cannot help but smile when I see you, or how you have managed to haunt my every thought." His voice came out hoarse with emotion. "Please explain why I cannot comprehend a life without you." He touched the side of her face, in awe at the hope in her eyes. He could not let the light burn out within them. He had almost convinced her. His gaze fell to her lips, his father's words echoing in his mind. *Kiss her.*

Before his nerve could flee, he leaned down, dropping his other hand from the window, taking her face between both his hands. He searched her eyes, seeking permission there. Her gaze fell to his mouth briefly before she took a swift and unexpected step backward.

"I must go," she said in a soft voice.

"Amelia," he reached for her as she hurried past, but she did not stop until she had escaped through the doorway. He leaned against the window pane, cursing himself for being so forward with her. Why had he tried to kiss her? He had frightened her away for good.

He leaned his forearm against the glass, a deep ache penetrating his heart. She would never find it within her to care for him. He had confessed his feelings, and she had run from him. Why had he allowed himself to hope it could be any different?

He could not face his father now. He could not stay in the house for another moment. With large strides, he walked down the hall and out the front door. A light breeze stirred the air as he made his way to the nearby ocean. The sun had just begun to set, streaking the sky in various orange hues. The ocean was the only place he could think clearly. Between the sea and a pile of stones to throw, he could only hope his emotions could be put back in their proper place by the day's end. Although her actions suggested otherwise, he couldn't deny what he had seen in Amelia's eyes.

She was starting to believe.

Adam clung to that hope as he tossed a heavy stone into the crashing waves.

Chapter 13

*A*melia had scarcely stopped to breathe on her way home from her meeting with Adam. Her legs shook as she came upon her small house, and she paused to collect herself before entering through the door. Why was she such a coward? Adam had nearly kissed her and she had—quite literally—run away. She placed a hand on her cheek, still feeling the gentle touch of Adam there, burning under her skin. She had never been so affected by a man in her entire life.

She leaned against the door, her face spreading into a smile. He had confessed that he cared for her. She had never heard sweeter words than the ones that he had spoken to her in the library. Her fear had been irrational, yes, but Amelia was beginning to wonder if love was not so irrational after all.

The stirring in her heart told a story, whispering into

her mind that the things she felt for Adam were real. That perhaps those things might last longer than a brief infatuation. How terrible she must have made him feel by running away. She bit her lip, gazing out at the sea beyond her small house. Tomorrow she would find him again. She would tell him that she might consider taking a chance at love. Her entire body flooded with warmth and contentment as she pulled open the door.

"Aunt Margaret!" Amelia called into the open space. Her eyes caught on Fanny, sitting on the sofa, a look of worry drawn over her youthful features.

"Miss Margaret is in her room," Fanny said in a quiet voice. "I'm afraid she is very distraught. I do not know how to appease her."

Amelia frowned, walking farther into the room. "What has happened?" she whispered.

Fanny shook her head, her eyes wide with concern. "She did not wish to speak of it."

Amelia moved down the hall and found Aunt Margaret's door to be closed. She tapped her knuckles against it. "May I come in?"

A squeak and a sniff were the only response Amelia heard. Taking it as a confirmation, she turned the handle. As Aunt Margaret came into view, Amelia's heart sunk to her feet. She lay on her bed, her cheeks red and streaked with tears, several soiled handkerchiefs strewn around her. Amelia froze where she stood, pressing her hand to her chest. All elation and joy that she had felt upon entering the house fled from her at the sight of her aunt in such disarray.

"What is the matter?" Amelia breathed.

Aunt Margaret bit back another stream of tears, clutching her throat with one hand. "Mr. B-Booth never c-cared for me at all. He—he only pretended in order to d-deceive me. He and his friends—they made a fool of me, Amelia." She covered her face, falling back onto her pillows.

Amelia rushed forward, sitting on the edge of her aunt's bed. Hot anger coursed through her as she tried to make sense of what she heard.

Aunt Margaret rubbed her nose, taking a steadying breath. "When Mr. Booth's carriage arrived for me today, he s-set the horses in motion before I could enter the carriage. He w-watched as I attempted to run after the carriage, and that was when I heard them laughing. An entire group of cruel men from within the carriage! They meant to mock me for my leg." She squeezed her eyes shut, keeping further tears from escaping.

Shocked at first, Amelia now seethed.

"I was wrong to believe that men could be worth a thought, or worth any piece of my heart." Aunt Margaret gave a hard laugh, wiping a tear from her cheek. "How could I have been so daft? I shall never make that mistake again."

Amelia's mind spun and her stomach twisted with dread. How dare this Mr. Booth be so cruel? How dare he toy with Aunt Margaret's heart in such a despicable way? His mockery alone would have been enough to set Amelia's blood boiling, but that he had broken her heart in the process? He would not escape unscathed, Amelia would make sure of that. Leaning forward, she wrapped her arms around her aunt, allowing her to cry on her shoulder.

There was little Amelia could say that would comfort her aunt. How could Amelia pretend to understand how a rejection of such hateful circumstances felt? Her heart ached as she listened to her aunt's weeping. Amelia knew it was not just for this instance that Aunt Margaret cried.

It was every time she had given hope to love and seen it crash down upon her, bringing increasing pain with each blow.

Amelia blinked back her own tears, feeling her own hope crashing down like lightning. Amelia had seen her mother snubbed by the man meant to love and care for her. She had heard one tale of heartbreak from her aunt, and had now witnessed another firsthand. Perhaps it was best to keep her heart hidden, to live her life without the trouble of a man. She had come to that conclusion long ago, and until recently it had been an easy rule to live by. Until Adam.

When Aunt Margaret pulled away from their embrace, she wiped her nose messily on her arm, slapping the tears from her swollen eyes. "No man is worth my tears."

Amelia shook her head. "Not one," she said, wiping a stray tear from her aunt's chin.

Amelia set her jaw. Mr. Booth would have a few tears of his own to shed when Amelia was through with him. Her teeth clenched along with her fists.

"Would you please take a trip to the dipper with me on the morrow?" Aunt Margaret asked again, her voice raw.

Amelia looked at her with as much sincerity as she could muster. "I would be honored. But please do not allow a pathetic man such as Mr. Booth to discount your worth. What is found within you is greater than anything the Brighton waters can cure. Mr. Booth's wicked nature could not be cured if the entire ocean were forced down his throat."

Aunt Margaret's eyes wobbled with tears once again, and she wrapped Amelia in a hug so firm she could scarcely breathe.

"No man is worth your tears," Amelia reminded her.

Aunt Margaret pulled back, squeezing Amelia's cheek.

"These tears are for you and your precious heart. You are worth an entire ocean of tears to me."

Amelia gripped her hand, a fierce protection overcoming her for this aunt she loved so dearly.

That night as Amelia lay in bed, her body refused to sleep, her mind racing with doubt. She could not allow her heart to come in the way of her head. She had claimed to be intelligent, but allowing herself to become attached to a man was not intelligent at all. She had seen the destruction of love and all matters of deceit one could place upon another's heart. She had been a witness of the destruction of love and she had been guilty of it with Lord Ramsbury. Her stomach writhed with wrongdoing. Was she so different from Mr. Booth?

She wanted no part of it any longer. No part of deceit, no part of lies, no part of betrayal, and no part of love.

The sun had just begun splitting the clouds when Amelia and Aunt Margaret made their way to the beach to be dipped once again. Amelia's eyes were stinging and puffy from lack of sleep, and while Aunt Margaret claimed the waters would revive them, Amelia could only guess that the salt of the ocean would contribute to the sting. But in an effort to maintain her aunt's lifted spirits, Amelia agreed with her wholeheartedly.

Her mind and heart felt numb from overuse and anxiety as they were pulled into the ocean in their bathing machines. When Amelia came to her dipper, she realized it was the same woman that had dipped her previously. The elderly woman eyed her for a long moment, pulling her by the arm into the water. "You seem to be suffering a different ailment than before."

Amelia scowled. "I suffer from nothing."

The woman tsked, taking Amelia's chin between her thumb and index finger, turning her head from side to side, peering into her eyes as if she could see her soul there. "You suffer from another bout of worry and fear. You are also ailing with a broken heart, I see."

Amelia shook her head. "No, I—"

"Thirty dips."

"What—"

Before Amelia could finish, the woman began her dipping, and Amelia felt the familiar struggle for breath as she was forced into the water and brought up again.

No less than thirty times.

Feeling very much like a drowned rodent, Amelia climbed back into the bathing machine, dazed and not at all surprised to find her eyes stinging profusely. She pushed back a pile of soaked hair from her face, spitting out water.

"Don't hide from your feelings, miss. You'll only bring suffering upon yourself and the one you care for."

A shiver ran over Amelia's skin as she changed into dry clothing. She did not know if the shiver came from her wetness or the fact that the dipper had seemed to read her mind.

Aunt Margaret was waiting for Amelia when she found her way to the shore, sitting in the sand. She stood, smiling enough to draw a smile from Amelia. "The condition of my leg has not changed, but my spirits have been lifted, to be sure. I was quite entertained watching you endure your thorough dipping." Aunt Margaret snorted.

"I am glad to hear it," Amelia said. She wished she could

say the same about her own spirits. Guilt still plagued her, and she knew the time had come to reveal her ruse to Lord Ramsbury. She could think of nothing else. Any thought of Adam that passed her defenses was quickly cast out. If she was going to commit to a life without deceit, she needed to make right her wrongdoings, starting with Lord Ramsbury.

At noon that day, once Amelia's hair had dried and been styled by Fanny, she set out to the assembly rooms, knowing that Lord Ramsbury would be there to see her. Her heart thumped with dread, but she knew what she needed to do.

When she entered through the first doors, she found Lord Ramsbury leaned against a nearby wall, surrounded by a group of extravagantly dressed people. He wore a yellow waistcoat with several fobs, rehearsing a story to a crowd that listened with eager ears. Amelia waited behind them until Lord Ramsbury's eyes found her. He stopped, excusing himself from the group, and walked toward her. His face lit up in a smile, his eyes sweeping over her face like a caress. "Miss Amelia." His words stopped there, his smile spreading impossibly wider. "I have missed you."

"You saw me just yesterday, my lord."

"The day passed like an eternity without you." He took her hand, pulling her toward him. "Come, allow me to introduce you to my friends. They have heard much about you and have been begging to make your acquaintance."

Her chest tightened with panic. "No, I cannot. There is something I must speak with you about. It cannot be delayed." She couldn't allow him to introduce her to his friends only for him to later learn that their brief courtship had been nothing but a lie.

He glanced over his shoulder before tipping he head

closer to hers. "What is the matter?" His blue eyes filled with concern that plucked at her heartstrings.

There were a small number of things she had learned about Lord Ramsbury in the short time she had known him, but most importantly she had learned that he was not entirely the wealthy and arrogant scoundrel he pretended to be among the public. And that made it even more difficult to say the things she would have to say.

"May we speak outside?" She swallowed.

"Yes, of course." He took her hand, wrapping it around his arm, guiding her through the doors and into the warmth of the sun. The blue sky matched Lord Ramsbury's eyes as he looked down at her, an array of questions burning within his gaze.

Amelia stepped away from him, taking a deep breath. She could not look at him for fear of what she might find in his eyes. "I have not been honest with you." She stared at a twig that rested near her feet.

"Nor have I." Lord Ramsbury's voice, deep and serious, brought her gaze back to his. Could he mean he had not been honest about Eleanor? Her heart thudded.

"I cannot bear to keep secrets from you any longer," he said.

Amelia took a step closer, anticipation burning within her. She would finally learn the truth about Eleanor. If her ruse was going to end, she could at least receive her prize of information.

"I have not been forthright with my intentions toward you," he said. Her stomach flipped. "My feelings for you are strong and unyielding. I cannot deny the happiness that has filled my life since the moment I first met you. I daresay there will never be another woman that I can envision spending my life with." He drew closer, stealing

Amelia's hand again. "Will you consider giving me the honor of becoming my wife?"

Amelia couldn't breathe. Shock spread through her limbs, clouding her mind with confusion. When she realized what had just happened, she felt very near to casting up her accounts all over Lord Ramsbury's perfect boots. She jerked her hand away without thinking.

"I am honored that you would say such things." Amelia's voice shook. "But I cannot accept your proposal."

His face fell.

"I am not all you profess me to be. I am not deserving of the life you promise me. I have deceived you." She breathed out fast, blinking back the tears that stung her eyes.

Lord Ramsbury's eyes flashed with hurt, and he crossed his arms over his chest, as if to hold his heart together. He didn't speak, but the confusion on his face pushed Amelia forward with her confession.

"I do not know Eleanor Claridge, but I know her brother. When I overheard you while engaged in a conversation that involved her, I resolved to help her family find her by any means necessary. I knew you possessed information that may lead to her discovery." She dropped her gaze to the ground when she saw the pain building in his eyes. "My one design in my attention toward you was to uncover your knowledge of Eleanor. I do not return your feelings. I am sorry."

The air between them hummed with silence for several seconds, and Amelia finally dared a glance at his face. She didn't know what she expected. Perhaps anger, betrayal, or hatred. But what she saw was a pitiful sorrow in his eyes, broken things hovering there.

Lord Ramsbury, the odious flirt—the arrogant, devil-may-care man, had a heart after all.

And Amelia had broken it.

"Leave me," he said in a whisper, casting his eyes upon the ground, rubbing the sole of his boot in the space between cobblestones. His jaw tightened.

Amelia's heart ached with regret. "I am very sorry." She wanted to ask one last time for the truth, but she couldn't bring herself to do so.

His eyes met hers one more time before he turned his back to her, walking away from the assembly room.

Amelia did not feel the relief she had expected to feel. She only felt guilt and shame so heavy she could hardly bear it. Love was indeed real. It was real, but it was destructive. It was real, but it was dangerous.

She felt like a failure in every way. Adam still planned to help her win her bargain with her father, but she had done little to help him find Eleanor. Did she even want to win the bargain with her father? To do so would mean more lies and deceit. She had been learning that those things were treacherous and wrong. At any rate, she didn't deserve Adam's help. All her attempts to assist him in finding Eleanor had quickly gone awry, leaving a trail of betrayal.

With a heavy heart, she set off toward the nearby coast, secretly hoping she might find Adam there. She had resolved to stay away from him, but her heart ached with longing to see him, to be near him. And she was weak.

But he would be disappointed in her for giving up Lord Ramsbury, their last resource for finding Eleanor. He would hate her for it. He might even refuse to fulfill his end of their arrangement. Amelia's stomach sunk at the thought of returning home to Nottingham and marrying Mr. Clinton. She knew deep in her bones that if the day came that she was forced to marry, her choice would be Adam.

But because of their false engagement, that day would never come. The point of the arrangement, after all, was that she would never have to marry. She could remain unmarried for her entire life, just like Aunt Margaret. To allow herself to fall in love felt like a betrayal to her aunt when the woman had suffered so much at the hands of love.

Amelia found a quiet area of the beach where few people had gathered. The coast was rocky here, and she lifted her skirts to avoid tripping on the stones. Finding a large rock, she sat down, gazing out at the ocean that appeared to extend forever. But she knew there was a point that it ended, meeting land in a far off place that she couldn't see.

"It's beautiful." A familiar voice made her heart leap. Her eyes slid to her left as Adam came to sit on a rock beside her.

As if acting of its own will, her mouth twisted in a wry smile. "Is this meeting a coincidence or have you been following me?"

He laughed, his dark hair falling over his brow, contrasting with the pale blue color of his eyes. "It seems we are both drawn to the ocean when we are seeking peace."

Amelia couldn't let him discover that she had come here seeking him. She had begun to wonder that if the Brighton waters did *not* hold magical power, that Adam did. Already she could feel the discontent and sorrow being drawn out of her heart. She didn't want to tell him what had happened with Lord Ramsbury. Not today. She could not bear his disappointment when she needed his support so much.

"I wondered if you might help me with a small quest," Amelia said.

He raised an eyebrow in question.

"The man my aunt met at the ball has proved himself to be a boor of the most despicable sort. I declare him worthy of revenge, and I thought you might assist me."

Adam laughed before realizing Amelia was indeed serious. "What has he done?"

"He made a mockery of my aunt and broke her heart." Amelia relayed the rest of the details that Aunt Margaret had told her. Adam listened, his own jaw tightening with anger.

"What do you suggest we do?" he asked.

She turned to him, grinning. "He wears a wig. Aunt Margaret told me he is ashamed of his baldness."

"We must take the wig."

"Precisely."

Adam rubbed his hands together, a childish excitement shining his his eyes. "What is this man's name?"

She sighed. "That is the quandary, I'm afraid. I have not seen him so I may not be able to recognize him. His name is Mr. Booth."

Adam jerked his gaze to her. "I know Mr. Booth!"

"Do you?"

He narrowed his eyes. "You are right, he is a dreadful man. Anything he can do to gain attention, honorable or not, he will do it."

"Do you know where we might find him?" Amelia asked.

"He will be at the ball tonight, to be sure. He would never miss an opportunity to be seen by the public."

She gritted her teeth, shaking her head in disgust. "He will regret hurting my aunt."

Adam's lips pressed together as if holding back a laugh. His shoulders shook.

"What?" she snapped, still thinking of her hatred of Mr. Booth.

"I never imagined you could look so . . . angry."

She crossed her arms. "No one hurts my aunt and escapes with their dignity. Or in Mr. Booth's case, his hair."

Adam collapsed in laughter, excitement shining in his eyes. Amelia laughed until her stomach hurt, forgetting any previous resolve she might have had against enjoying her time with Adam. A strong sense of belonging enveloped her as she sat on the rocks, laughing with him.

Several minutes later, with their plan concocted, Amelia stood up. "Shall we go?"

Adam shook his head. "The ball will not begin for another hour at least."

Amelia cast her eyes heavenward, where the sky showed its colors of deep blue and purple. The sun had disappeared beneath the horizon, darkness hiding behind the clouds. She sat down again, glancing at Adam's face beside her. The last time they had been together he had nearly kissed her. Her eyes flickered to his closed-lipped smile. She swallowed, moving her gaze to her hands in her lap.

"I wonder where Eleanor could be," she whispered, gazing out at the seemingly endless sky. "Do you believe Miss Reed and Lord Ramsbury? Do you believe she might have run away?"

A sadness flooded Adam's eyes, making Amelia regret asking. "I do not want to believe it, but when I consider the alternative, that she might have been abducted or harmed, I find great peace in the possibility." He looked down, a furrow in his brow.

Amelia had never given similar thought to the situation. Seeing Adam now, with his eyes cast down and filled with worry, her heart thumped with grief. She had always hated to see the sorrow in his expression. Without considering the dangers of doing so, she reached out and touched his arm. His gaze found hers in the dimness, and she found herself trapped in it. If only she had the courage to admit to him that perhaps she had been wrong. If only she had the courage to take his face in her hands and kiss him, just as she had stopped him from doing the day before. There was something about the nearby ocean with its swaying musical waves and the enchanting colors of evening painted across the sky that heightened every whisper of her heart. Every longing.

"We will find Eleanor," she said in a whisper. "And we will avenge my aunt."

Adam smiled, and Amelia's heart threatened to burst. "What an ambitious pair we make."

She silently agreed, holding hostage the words she meant to say. She knew Adam cared for her. He had confessed such in the library the day before. So why did she find it so terrifying to speak aloud the feelings in her own heart? A small part of her still doubted that they could be true.

In the hour that followed, they spoke of lighter things, laughing until their stomachs ached. Amelia drew pictures in the sand, and since drawing had never been a talent of hers, Adam found them vastly amusing. By the time the sky had fully faded to darkness, Adam suggested they find their way to the ballroom.

Inside, as suspected, they found Mr. Booth among a crowd of spectators. Amelia grimaced at his smug face, lined with wrinkles and finished with a brown wig and a top hat. Adam had agreed to the most difficult part of their plan. He would offer Mr. Booth a flute of champagne, and Amelia would walk past, 'accidentally' colliding with Adam, causing him to fall, taking Mr. Booth's wig and top hat to the ground with him.

The plan went through without a single mistake. As Mr. Booth's wig fell to the ground, he clutched his head, ducking away from the gasping faces of the crowd. Amelia rushed out the ballroom door, laughing until she was breathless. Adam followed, taking her by the hand as they ran away from the light of the assembly rooms.

"Aunt Margaret will be pleased," Amelia said through her laughter.

"Shall we see her now? I have a gift for her." He help up the shiny, oiled wig between two fingers.

Amelia couldn't contain her dismay. "I thought you left it on the floor!"

"I thought your aunt might require proof of our nefarious endeavor."

Amelia could scarcely breathe, her laughter stealing every bit of air from her lungs. She finally choked out, "Aunt Margaret does not require proof to believe anything at all."

Adam gave her hand a squeeze before releasing it to her side. "You might consider adopting that quality."

Her gaze darted to his face, but he did not meet her eyes. "Are you suggesting that I learn to believe in the cure of the Brighton waters?" Amelia asked. But she knew what he really spoke of. Her heart beat fast, hoping he would ask her—hoping he would give her the courage to speak the things in her heart.

He gave her a half smile, but his eyes were heavy. He did not answer. He knew that Amelia had understood his meaning.

The remainder of their walk passed in silence, her jovial mood imposed upon by Adam's words. When the house came into view, they walked up the steps, and Amelia pushed open the door. Aunt Margaret sat on the sofa beside Fanny, decorating a new bonnet with trim.

"Mr. Claridge!" she exclaimed, pushing herself to her feet. "What are you doing with my niece at such an hour? Alone in the darkness of evening, no less." She gave him a half-hearted glare, a smile hovering behind her eyes.

He held up one hand in surrender, keeping the other tucked behind his back, hiding the wig from her view. With great effort, Amelia managed to conceal her grin.

"I was merely helping your niece exact vengeance on your behalf," he said, walking farther into the room. With a flourish, Adam pulled the wig out from behind his back, tossing it toward Aunt Margaret.

She caught it with a screech before throwing it to the ground, scrambling onto the sofa. Fanny flung herself to the opposite end of the cushions to avoid being sat upon. Aunt Margaret pressed her hand to her chest, her cheeks flushed. "What the devil is that? Did you dare bring a rodent into this house?"

Amelia erupted in laughter and Adam joined her, bending over at the waist.

"What *is* it?" With apprehension in her eyes, Aunt Margaret touched one foot to the ground, leaning toward the limp wig with squinted eyes.

When Amelia could finally breathe enough to speak, she said, "It is the hair of Mr. Booth. He has experienced the flavor of his own wicked ways. Adam—er—Mr. Claridge performed the honor of knocking it from Mr. Booth's arrogant head."

Aunt Margaret's eyes grew so wide that Amelia wondered if they would fall onto the floor beside the wig. Was she angry? The silence in the air was excruciating.

Pushing herself to her feet, Aunt Margaret crossed the room to Adam. With a wobbling chin, she pinched his cheek, planting a noisy kiss upon it. "Bless you, boy."

He stood back in shock, and Amelia stifled another laugh. With a boisterous hoot, Aunt Margaret fell back onto the cushions of the sofa, laughing until her face burned bright red.

"You have restored my faith in men, my dear," she managed, wiping tears of mirth from her blue eyes. "I have half a mind to marry you myself, but I will leave Amelia to that."

Amelia gasped, throwing her aunt a look of consternation. Her cheeks grew hot as her aunt chuckled. She refused to look at Adam's face.

"There is no need to tarnish this lovely night with talk of marriage," Amelia said with a laugh. But it seemed of the small party in the room, she was the only one to find her words humorous at all. Aunt Margaret opened her mouth to speak. Amelia cringed, hoping she would not embarrass her further.

"Will you favor us with a reading, Miss Amelia?" Fanny interrupted in a quick voice. Amelia threw her a look of gratitude. Fanny continued, returning Amelia's smile, "I quite enjoy your expression in reading poetry."

"Of course." Amelia moved to a chair beside the sofa, and Adam took the one by the fireplace across the room.

The rest of the evening was spent in more laughter, poetry, and conversation. Amelia even convinced Fanny to sing a song. Her voice was crisp and beautiful. Amelia's heart soared with more joy and contentment than she had ever felt before. She had never laughed so much in one evening; she was sure of it. And at the moments her eyes found Adam's across the room, she did not tear them away. She smiled at him, exchanging words without sound.

When Adam took his leave, Amelia almost followed him out the door. Her courage was fleeting, and she needed to tell him that his words to her in the library had not been in vain. She could not promise him her heart, but she could promise him that he had awoken something within her—a belief in something that had once seemed impossible, irrational, and far beyond her capability. But there was still a small seed within her that writhed and ached, begging her to remember the neglect in her mother's face and the coldness in her father's, the pain in Aunt Margaret's voice, and the broken things in Lord Ramsbury's eyes.

So she stayed in her chair, keeping her mouth closed against the things she wanted to say. As the door swung shut behind him, Amelia felt the sharpness of Aunt Margaret's gaze on her cheek. She turned, one eyebrow raised in question.

"I expect you will choose the third option now," her aunt said, crossing her arms with a stern look of reprimand.

"I don't understand ..."

"When you enter into your false engagement with Mr. Claridge, you will not break the engagement in a proper manner, nor will you falsify his death. You will marry him."

Amelia sputtered, turning in her chair. "I never wish to marry."

"Nonsense, child. I said such things too in my youth, but I did not mean them. I have said such things to you, but I did not mean them. I only aspired to spinsterhood because I knew it was likely the only hand fate had dealt me." She waved a finger at Amelia, her voice growing louder. "You have a kind, honest, caring man that loves you. Do not toss him to the wind because you have your pride to maintain. Do not doubt the thing which hovers right before your eyes. Do you remember the list we made upon our departure from Nottingham?"

Amelia exhaled, her emotions sneaking to the surface, stinging her eyes with unexpected tears. "Yes."

They had made a list of all the things Amelia wanted a man to be. She remembered the qualities written there, but not before Aunt Margaret hobbled to her bedchamber and retrieved the list, setting it on Amelia's lap to read. Most of the words, all but 'Lord Lovely,' had been crossed out lightly, but she could still read them.

Not ridiculous.
Charming, kind, patient.
Handsome, much younger than Mr. Clinton, mature.
Honest, intelligent, gentle, and entertaining.
Positively lovely.

In his own way, Adam filled each of these roles with ease. Aside from being slightly ridiculous. She smiled to herself, looking up at her aunt. "Why is it so very difficult?"

"You have a bit of my stubbornness within you, I'm afraid."

Amelia laughed. "But I can only hope to one day possess a portion of your strength."

Aunt Margaret's chin wobbled before her face contorted into a scowl. "How dare you make me cry." She took her cane from where it rested against the tea table, wagging it at Amelia with a compressed smile. She stood to retire for the evening. Fanny followed her to her room, leaving only one candle to light the small sitting room where Amelia remained.

She stared at the flame as it burned, captivated by the various shades of orange and yellow. Her aunt's words streamed through her mind, branching down to her heart, filling it with strength. Tomorrow she would find Adam and tell him how she felt. The thought made her chest clench with fear. She shook it away, jumping to her feet and taking the candle with her down the hall to her room. Her heart fluttered with excitement and terror all at once.

With a smile painted on her lips, she changed into her nightdress without waiting for Fanny's assistance. As she settled into her blankets, peace permeated her soul. She did not think of her failure, her doubt, or the disheartening truth that Eleanor was still to be found. She only thought of Adam, and the new hope and belief that bloomed inside her.

Chapter 14

A letter arrived for Amelia the next morning, a long missive that appeared to have been passed under the door, the wax seal glowing under the morning sun. She opened the door, peering out at the surrounding area, before closing it with a frown. Who might have dropped a letter at their door?

Amelia had hardly slept the night before, eager to find Adam that day. She had awoken early, already dressed and ready to leave when she had found the letter. The quiet of the house only intensified her curiosity as she sat down at the table and tore the seal, unfolding the parchment with shaking hands. Her eyes jumped to the signature. Lord Ramsbury.

The writing was small and neat, spreading out over the entire page. Her heart raced as her eyes scanned over the first paragraph.

Dear Miss Buxton,

It is my intention, through this letter, to reveal to you all I know of Miss Eleanor Claridge. I could not, in good conscience, keep the truth from you any longer. I betray a dear friend in doing so, and I ask that you keep me secret as your source of enlightenment. Her family and friends deserve to know what she has done.

Amelia read the rest, all the way to the bottom of the page, covering her mouth in astonishment. Her thoughts spun as she sat back in her chair, trying to make sense of what she had just read. Leaping up from her chair, she whisked the letter from the table before rushing out the door to find Adam.

Adam looked into the eyes of his reflection, tying his cravat loosely. His hair stood up at strange angles, and his eyes were puffy from lack of sleep. He pressed his hair down and rubbed his eyes. Amelia had haunted his dreams and every waking thought since the night before. He smiled to himself, thinking of the enjoyment they had shared over her aunt's revenge. He had never found it so easy to laugh, especially at such a difficult time of his life.

His father had spent much of the night coughing, another reason Adam had not slept. The coughing had taken on a different sound as the night wore on. A weaker, dryer sound. Little time remained for him to live, and it choked Adam with grief. When his father was gone, Adam would have nothing. No parents, no siblings, and soon no Amelia. A few months from now she would return to Nottingham and he would write to her father, requesting her hand in marriage. He would accompany her to Nottingham, but when the time came, he would bid Amelia farewell forever. He clenched his jaw against the turmoil within him. Had her feelings changed? He shook away the thought, unwilling to hope for unlikely things.

"Adam," the hoarse voice of his father barely reached him from down the hall. He moved to the door, pulling it open.

"Father?"

"I am in the drawing room." There was something odd about his father's voice.

With large strides, Adam hurried down the hall and through the door of the drawing room. His father sat on the settee, his shaking hand holding what appeared to be a letter.

"From Eleanor." His father looked up, a mixture of emotions in his eyes.

Adam's heart picked up speed, his breath catching. "Eleanor? Are you certain?" His voice came out weak.

"It is written in her hand."

Adam sat down beside his father, trying to read the emotions on his face, desperately hoping to find relief there. All he saw was concern, confusion, and a bit of astonishment. The letter lay open on his lap, resting in his shaking hands. The writing could not be mistaken for any other hand but Eleanor's. Adam would recognize the loops and lines anywhere.

He held his breath before saying in a hesitant voice, "May I read it?"

His father extended the letter to Adam, his eyes glazed. Adam took the parchment from his father's hand, his heart pounding so loudly he could hardly focus on the words that blurred beneath his gaze.

Dear Papa,

There is little I can say to you in the way of apology, for I know I do not deserve your forgiveness, nor do I ask for it. I also do not ask for your understanding, but only that you receive this missive and know that I am alive, and I am happy. I write now as I ride to London, where I will marry Mr. William Quinton. I love Mr. Quinton, and I know he will bring me exceeding happiness. Knowing that you did not approve of him and would never endorse the match, I aspired to escape in secret. My reputation will be safe as well as the Claridge name, not to worry. Suspecting you or per-haps Adam may follow me to London, I was forced to keep my departure a secret, as was Mr. Quinton, until we had secured our marriage.

I confided in but two trusted friends, Miss Darby and Miss Reed. Please do not blame them for fulfilling their promise of silence to me. Mr. Quinton confided in one man of the regiment, and another man of his acquaintance.

I shall think of you and Adam often. Please do not come searching for me, for I do not wish to return to Brighton. I regret the worry and unease I have caused you, and wish you all the best in your recovery to good health. I cannot give you the address in which I will receive your letters, but I will promise to write you upon occasion.

With love and sincerity,

Eleanor

Adam reread the words. He did not know how he expected to feel. But the anger that boiled in his heart surprised him. He threw the letter to the ground, jumping to this feet. His vision clouded with heat as he paced the room. How could Eleanor have willingly put their father through such pain and distress? Did she think this... *letter* could reverse that? Did she not realize that he would be dead soon? Adam tried to remember this Mr. Quinton, but only recalled seeing him once. He and Eleanor had never acted in any manner suggesting an attachment.

"You knew this Mr. Quinton?" Adam asked, his voice sharp. "How could Eleanor leave us without a word?"

"Adam, sit down." His father's voice was stern and broken at once.

He turned and sat with reluctance, resting his forehead in his hands. His mind spun, stealing his focus from his father's words.

"All I wish for is Eleanor's happiness. I did not find Mr. Quinton to be deserving of Eleanor when I first made his acquaintance, but he has managed to make her happy. That is all I can hope for." He pushed himself to his feet with great effort, shuffling back toward his bedchamber.

Adam frowned at his father's retreating frame. "You cannot be serious. Think of the suffering she has inflicted upon us! Think of the hours of turmoil we've suffered as we searched for a girl that did not wish to be found." He seethed with anger and his heart burned. His father continued walking. Adam heard the soft click of a door, knowing it was the door to his father's bedchamber, where he would likely release the emotions he had been holding back in front of Adam. His father had always been strong and unyielding, a beacon of fortitude. In his dying state, with a broken and grieving heart, he had become something Adam did not recognize. His father still tried to be strong, but the effort only made him weaker. And Eleanor had played the largest role in that.

Adam worked through the details of Eleanor's letter in his mind, struggling to make sense of them. Lord Ramsbury had been Mr. Quinton's other confidant. And the first must have been the soldier Amelia had seen Lord Ramsbury speaking with in the assembly room. Miss Darby and Miss Reed had kept Eleanor's secret too. Miss Darby had not been concerned about her friend because she knew Eleanor had *chosen* to abandon her dying father.

All the clues fell into place. Adam couldn't believe he had been blind enough to miss the truth. But there it was, written in Eleanor's hand, clear and without mercy. Had he missed something? She had never exhibited a single sign of hatred toward Brighton, or discontent within their home. Eleanor had never seemed to be one that would fall prey to the charms of a man so suddenly. He had always assumed his sister to be more intelligent than that, but it now seemed that he never knew her true character at all. How selfish and cruel could a person be to leave their father in such devastation?

"Master Adam. There is a Miss Buxton here. She claims to have an urgent matter to discuss with you." Mr. Weston, their butler, stood in the doorway, rigid and uncomfortable in his stance. Surely he had a sense of Adam's unrest.

Adam stood. What could Amelia be doing here? His stomach sunk as he realized that he would have to tell her what had happened to Eleanor. Without the mystery of his sister's disappearance to uncover, there was nothing keeping Amelia at his side. And when he could see her again it would only be brief, pretend, and hopeless. Then she would be gone forever, just like Eleanor.

Adam doubted his heart could bear it.

Amelia stepped into the doorway, her brows drawn together in concern. She wore a gown the color of cream, trimmed with gold ribbon, making her eyes shine despite the anxiety within them. He scolded himself for admiring her, for wishing he could take her in his arms and never let her go. He was tired of hoping.

"What is the matter?" she asked, taking a hurried step into the room. Just as he had deciphered the unrest in her expression, she had seen the pain in his. "What has happened?"

"We have received word from Eleanor," he said in a quiet voice.

She covered her mouth with a gasp. "Is she well? Is she safe? Has her marriage escaped ridicule?"

Adam paused, scowling in confusion. "How did you know that Eleanor married?"

Amelia held up a folded piece of parchment. "Lord Ramsbury wrote this to me, a confession of all he knew concerning Eleanor and Mr. Quinton." Her voice came out breathless.

He rubbed a hand over his hair, drawing a deep breath. "It is settled, then. I did not expect Eleanor to be so dull-witted and selfish. I might not have spent so much time in search of her if I had known she could so willingly bring our family to despair. She means to never return." He shook his head. "I was so certain of her happiness here in Brighton. I thought she loved us. It seems her infatuation with Mr. Quinton was stronger." His face twisted in disgust.

Amelia stepped toward him, the sympathy in her gaze enough to disarm him. The creases of worry in her forehead, the gentle down turning of her brows and lips as she attempted to comfort him . . . it was all a fierce attack against his resolve to keep his heart. She touched his arm, and it was all he could do not to pull her to him and finish what he had started in the library.

"At least she is safe," Amelia said in a half-whisper.

The words grated on him. It sounded much like what his father had said. He turned away from her, crossing his arms over his chest.

Three clicks sounded on the floor as Amelia approached him from behind. Why must she torture him in such a way? He would not allow her to steal his heart any longer. He knew her intentions, and he knew they were not in his favor. He refused to be a chess piece in her elaborate game. His father needed him now more than ever, and he could not be distracted chasing a woman that did not want to be caught, a heart that did not want to be his. He had spent enough time already searching for something that did not want to be found.

"Is there something I might do to help you and your father?" Amelia's voice ached in his ears. He closed his eyes, keeping his back turned to her.

"You may leave us. Call upon me when you are prepared to leave for Nottingham and I will keep my word to you."

He heard her sharp intake of breath from behind him. "I am still here in Brighton for two months."

"Then I shall see you in two months." His voice came out colder than he intended. He immediately turned around, regret pouring through his chest.

Her eyes refused to meet his as she backed toward the door, her cheeks flushed. "Wish your father well from me, then," she said as she stepped into the hall, bringing the door to an abrupt close behind her.

Adam clenched his teeth as he listened her retreating footsteps. It was a sound that would likely haunt him forever—the sound of Amelia stepping out of his life and heart forever. Or at least until she became his intended. He swallowed the pain that enveloped his heart, aching all the way to his bones. He had lost Eleanor, he had lost Amelia, and soon he would lose his father. The anger he had been feeling toward Eleanor was twisting into grief within his heart, squeezing and stabbing until he could hardly breathe. Would he ever see her again? Could he forgive her if he did? Her choice to leave did not make sense.

There was little else life could take from him. As he sat down on the settee again, he felt hope sink within him like a stone cast into the ocean. Heavy, unfeeling, and never to be seen again.

Chapter 15

TWO MONTHS LATER

It had been five weeks since Adam's father had died, leaving behind an empty house and a cold son. At first Adam had turned to the ocean for peace, as he had many times before, but all he could think of was Amelia. In the last month he had been reminded, since his mother's death, what it truly meant to miss someone. He missed his father. He missed Eleanor.

And he missed Amelia.

Early in the mornings he took to the sea, hoping that he might find Amelia and her aunt there, laughing as he tossed stones into the waves. But all he found were unfamiliar faces, more tourists from around England come to experience the wonders of Brighton and the prince's acclaimed land.

Amelia had not come to him. He knew she would be returning to her home in Nottingham soon, and he would need to find her. The volume of visitors in Brighton had decreased with the temperature as summer drew to a close. Winds and rains picked up nearly every day, darkening Adam's mood even further.

One morning, he ventured to call upon his friend Philip. Of all the people he knew, Philip was the most reliable. If Adam was going to pour his sorrows out upon a person and not be mocked for it, Philip was the man.

"Claridge, how do you do?" Philip greeted him as he met him in the entry hall of his home. Philip lived on the south side of Brighton, in a quaint home of dark gray stone and small windows. He too lacked much in the way of family, with only a grandmother who lived in a neighboring house. Philip gave a solemn smile, and the sight felt strangely blinding to Adam, for he had not seen or felt a smile in a long time. His friend placed a hand on his shoulder, a genuine look in his expression. "Accept my sincere condolences on your behalf. I always respected your father."

Adam tried to pull his mouth into a smile, but it felt like a limp puppet without strings. The effort was futile. "Thank you, Honeyfield."

Philip ushered him inside. "How are you faring, my friend?"

Adam considered a wide array of responses, but settled on the most truthful of them all. "Terribly so."

With Philip's wide brown eyes staring at Adam in concern, he appeared very much like a horse, his dark hair falling to one side of his face. "I expected as much, but I did not expect you would admit it outright."

"Why not?" Adam's voice came off dull.

"You are not one to…" Philip waved his hands in the air, "express your feelings."

Adam took his own liberty to collapse on the red sofa, his gaze fixing on the pianoforte across the drawing room. "You are wrong. I expressed my feelings to the woman I love, and she rejected me."

Philip came into Adam's line of view, standing between him and the pianoforte. "The woman from the ballroom? The one Ramsbury had claimed?"

"Yes."

Philip shook his head. "A man of such rank and title is not one to be competed with. You might have spared yourself a fair load of disappointment."

"She does not care for Ramsbury," Adam said.

"Well, then, it is no wonder she did not care for you," Philip said, a teasing glint in his eyes. With a sigh, he sat beside Adam on the settee. "I mean to say she is a nod-cock if she refused you. Did you offer for her?"

Adam shook his head.

Philip jumped back to his feet. "You did not?" he exclaimed.

Philip didn't understand. He didn't know that Adam and Amelia would see one another soon, when Adam returned to keep his word on their bargain. They would be engaged without a proposal, without a commitment, and without reciprocal feelings. But something within Adam doubted that Amelia was completely indifferent. He had seen the way she looked at Lord Ramsbury in comparison to the way she had looked at him. He had seen the difference between the smiles she gave other men and the smiles she gave him. But even so, that did not change her beliefs. She had told him she did not believe in love or marriage. He had tried to change her mind, and he had failed.

"She does not ever wish to marry," Adam said.

"By George, Adam." Philip shook his head. "You ought to propose to her! She shall never know the extent of your feelings if you do not promise to be hers forever. Through her perspective, you might have been insincere." Philip puzzled for a moment. "How long has it been since you have seen her?"

"Two months."

"Two months?!" Philip shook his head in disapproval.

"What do you suggest I do?" Adam sat forward. His friend acted the part of dignified expert in love, when in practice he lost all confidence in the presence of a pretty lady. Yet Adam had come to Philip for advice. Never had he been so desperate for enlightenment, that even Philip Honeyfield could bring light to his darkened mind.

"If you declared your feelings for her, then disappeared for two months, I am certain she doubts your words. You must show your devotion through your actions, my friend. By begging for her hand in marriage."

The air in Adam's lungs became heavy. "When?"

"Today."

Adam sputtered. "Are you mad?"

"Think of it. You could be happily engaged on the morrow. Does that not sound divine?" Philip flashed Adam a quick grin before pointing at the door. "Now get out."

Adam's heart bounded, sending his muscles into panic. He had avoided Amelia the past two months in an effort to keep himself free of more heartache. He had held onto his knowledge that he would still see her again. To seek her out now, offer his heart and be hurt again would be too much to bear.

"Go." Philip laughed, pointing at the door a second time. With a shaking breath, Adam stood.

"Hurrah!" Philip shouted. "I had begun to wonder if your legs still functioned."

Adam threw Philip a glare that only made him laugh harder.

"May you meet success," Philip called through the door as he closed it behind Adam.

Outside the air was cool and wet, and miniscule drops of rain and seawater blew through the wind. Adam paused to collect his thoughts. Did he really intend to do this? What if she refused him? He would still have to carry on and pretend to be engaged to her. Adam could think of nothing more torturous. As if carried through the wind, his father's words came to his mind. *I will not die knowing my son has such a troubled heart. Nor will I die knowing my son to be so cowardly.*

Adam could almost see the smirk upon his father's face. *I suppose you are a coward after all.*

He was not a coward. His father would hate to see him so relenting. If the smallest part of Amelia cared for him at all, he would make sure he knew of it. And he would make absolutely certain his feelings for her. There would be no more room for doubt. He would know if Amelia loved him or not, and she would know for certain that he did not wish to spend another day without her.

With clenched fists, Adam found himself moving toward her house. With his father's and Philip's advice in mind, Adam knew he could not fail.

Resting on the window, the raindrops reminded Amelia

of tears, much like the ones that burned behind her eyes as she looked out at the ocean she would soon bid farewell. Her father had written a fortnight previous, inquiring of her progress toward her engagement. In truth, she had not known how to answer.

Amelia had never known a man to be as true to his word as Adam. He had said he would not see her for two months, and so he hadn't. She had not so much as caught a glimpse of him at the coast, or outside his home when she had begged Aunt Margaret to accompany her on a walk past. He had always been very skilled at hiding. She tried not to smile at the memory of him hiding in the bushes when she had fallen victim to Miss Darby's rage. She pushed the thought away. Those memories, she had learned over the past two months, only brought pain.

Amelia could only hope that, since Adam was indeed true to his word, he would return to her before her departure to Nottingham. She could not marry Mr. Clinton now, especially not now that she understood what it meant to love. She needed Adam to play the role he had promised, no matter how badly it pained her. It seemed she had been yet another victim of love's sting and deceit.

Amelia sat on a chair by the front window of their little house, with Aunt Margaret stitching embroidery on the sofa behind her. They had spent the last two months exploring Brighton, visiting the shops, dipping in the waters, and visiting the grand pavilion. Amelia had been looking forward to such excursions since the moment she arrived, and had enjoyed herself. But without Adam, the color had all but faded from her fascination with this town.

She rested her chin in her hand, counting the droplets as they collided with the glass. The rest of the world beyond the window was blurred, the different hues fading together. A black smudge appeared in the center of the window, moving closer to the house. She pulled away from the glass, squinting at the figure as it approached.

She fell off her chair.

"Amelia!" Aunt Margaret cried before bursting into laughter. "Have you been struck by lightning?"

She felt as though she had. Amelia sat up on the floor and peered with one eye over the windowsill, struggling to tame her racing heart. There, taking the first step to the front door, was Adam. Gathering her fortitude, she leapt to her feet, smoothing her hair in front of Aunt Margaret. "How horrendous do I look?"

Aunt Margaret stretched her neck around Amelia, attempting to see out the window.

"Mr. Claridge is here," Amelia squeaked. "What shall I do?"

Her aunt clutched her cane, getting to her feet to adjust Amelia's hair. "I knew he would return. You may not imagine it possible, but men can be as stubborn as you and me." She tucked a strand behind Amelia's ear before patting her cheek with force. "Now go, and do not let him speak a word before you have spoken the words you meant to say two months ago."

Amelia swallowed, choking on a breath. With Eleanor's discovery and Adam's proceeding aloofness toward her, she had never had the opportunity to tell him how she felt. But he was only arriving today to fulfill his end of the bargain they had made, she reminded herself.

She sat down on the sofa, willing herself to remain calm. Aunt Margaret rubbed circles on her back as they waited, reminding Amelia to breathe. After a minute had passed, she jumped to her feet, creeping to the window.

She had seen him taking the first step up to the door. What could be taking him so long?

Standing away from view, she glanced out the window. Adam stood five feet from the steps, pacing the cobblestones like a cat. She studied his face, overwhelmed by the familiarity of his handsome features. It had seemed like years rather than months since she had seen him.

"What the devil is he doing?"

Amelia hadn't noticed Aunt Margaret come to stand behind her. She met her aunt's wide eyes. "I haven't the slightest notion." She bit her lower lip.

"Perhaps you might meet him outside," Aunt Margaret suggested.

Amelia's heart gave a leap. She did not think herself capable of facing him. Not when he had avoided her for so long. She took one more look out the window before drawing a deep breath. "Very well."

Aunt Margaret gave her a light push as she moved toward the door. Amelia's hand froze on the handle. Before she could lose her nerve, she opened the door, stepping outside before daring to look up.

Adam stood in front of her, no more than five paces away. He wore black all the way from his dark hair to his boots. He must still be in mourning, she thought. Amelia had hoped to attend the burial service, but Adam had never extended an invitation. She released her grip on the door handle behind her, forcing herself to look at his face. His eyes created a sharp contrast of blue to the black of his clothing, capturing her gaze.

Her heart gave a distinct leap.

Before he could speak, Amelia forced her mouth to move. "I am very sorry to hear of your father's passing. I hope you are well." Her voice came out softer than she intended, almost lost in the mist of light rain and wind.

It was as if his eyes were adhered to her, unable to see anything else. "I am as you would expect." His lips twitched, trying to become a smile, but he drew a shaking breath instead. "Have you been well?"

She set her jaw, keeping her emotions from showing. How could he ask her such a question? Of course she had not been well. He had pushed her away the past two months, leaving her to wonder if he cared for her at all, or if love truly was a lie. Leaving her to wonder if she would be resigned to marry Mr. Clinton after all.

"I leave for Nottingham soon," she said, willing her voice to come out stronger. A sudden gust of wind hit her face, stealing her breath. She wrapped her arms around herself.

Adam took a stride closer, blocking the wind from her. Warmth spread through her limbs, touching her cheeks as he took another stride until he stood close enough to touch. "That is why I have come."

Her heart sank. So he had only come to fulfill his end of their bargain. He had not come because he missed her, or because he cared for her. She looked down, away from his eyes, her legs shaking. Against her will, her chin wobbled. "You have come to complete our false engagement. To declare your false affection to me, and your false desire to marry me." A tear slipped from her eye, streaking down her cheek. "It has always been false, hasn't it? You mustn't tell me now that I was wrong to believe you." She released a shaking breath. "That I was wrong to believe in love for the shortest moment."

His jaw tightened as he stared at her, a decision hovering in his gaze. His muscles tensed visibly. Before she could comprehend it, he filled the space between them in three paces, taking her face between his hands and kissing her.

His lips were gentle, slow, and deliberate, his kiss deepening as he threaded his fingers into her hair. Her shaking hands found the lapels of his jacket, pulling him closer as she found the courage to kiss him in return. Her heart ached and soared, tiny flecks of doubt beginning to dispel as Adam's lips moved over hers.

He pulled away, just enough to look in her eyes, pausing to wipe away the tears that had fallen on her cheeks as he kissed her. She exhaled, breathless, gazing into the streaks of blue and green in his eyes, in awe at the adoration that shone within them.

"I have no intention of fulfilling the first option of our bargain." He brushed a strand of hair behind her ear, his lips twisting into a smile, his eyes begging to be understood. "I intend to enter into an engagement with you Amelia, but I intend to marry you when it is finished." He took a deep breath. "If you will have me."

Amelia could hardly believe his words. They overwhelmed her, and though she expected to feel afraid, she could feel nothing but happiness. She laughed, tears of a very different sort spilling from her eyes as she nodded. She let out a choked sound, a mixture between a sob and a laugh and the word *yes*.

His mouth spread into a wide smile. "Are you certain?"

She nodded before reaching up, touching the side of his face. She couldn't speak. She could hardly see him through the tears that clouded her eyes and the squint her smile brought. He wrapped his arms around her, stealing another kiss, and another, kissing her tears until they were dry. Her heart overflowed with emotion, contentment, and raw joy. She was unable to comprehend what had just happened.

Adam wished to marry her, and not only as a ruse.

"I love you," he whispered. "I suspect I have loved you since the day you found me on the beach, giving me hope when I had none." He took her hand in his, pressing it to his chest.

Amelia closed her eyes, saving his words as a precious gift. She felt the steady pulse of his heart beneath his shirt, unable to understand how it could belong to her. Gratitude bloomed inside her but she pushed it away before she could turn into a watering pot again.

But something still troubled her. "Why did you stay away for these two months? I thought you never wished to see me again."

He shook his head. "I would never wish for that. Learning of Eleanor's secret and seeing my father's grief, it left me with a broken heart. I couldn't risk having it broken further." He took her face between his hands, locking her gaze with his. "I regret every moment I chose to distance myself from you. I am sorry . . . very sorry for the pain I caused you. I did not know you cared." He still looked surprised, unsure of Amelia's feelings toward him.

"I meant to tell you that day," she said in a quick voice.

"Tell me what?"

"That I might have loved you."

His eyes widened. "You cannot be serious."

She covered her mouth to hide her grin at his expense. "You might have allowed me to tell you."

"I would not have believed it." He gave a subtle shake of his head, his gaze sweeping over her face. "I cannot believe I was such a nodcock. I'm sorry, Amelia. I am so sorry."

"I do love you, Adam," she said. Even as the words escaped her, she felt the truth of them sinking into her heart and finding a home there. She gasped. "It's true. I believe I do."

He chuckled, taking a moment to smooth the pieces of her hair he had undone when he kissed her. As if he couldn't help it, he kissed her lips one last time. Wrapping her hand around his arm, he smiled. "Shall we go inside to tell your aunt the delightful news?"

Amelia shook her head. "I doubt there will be a need for that. She has been watching from the window this entire time, to be sure." She glanced behind her, not at all surprised to see a head of blonde curls ducking beneath the window pane. Amelia's cheeks burned, but she didn't care.

When they entered the house, Aunt Margaret scrambled to the sofa, a nonchalant smile pasted on her lips. She raised one eyebrow at Adam, her expression hardening. "How dare you snub us for two months? I was just beginning to grow fond of you."

He laughed. It seemed Adam had finally learned to understand the mirth behind Aunt Margaret's sardonic commentary. "Would I gain your favor once more if you knew that I will soon marry Amelia?"

Aunt Margaret let out a squeal, clapping her hands together. "I knew you were not a coward, Mr. Claridge. But you will do nothing of the sort until you have gained express permission from Amelia's father. Then we shall see a real show of your courage."

Oh, yes. If there was one negative thing that had come from this engagement, it was that Amelia's father would see himself to have succeeded. But she had not chosen Adam only to please her father, or simply to avoid Mr. Clinton. Her heart had chosen Adam without consulting her. She smiled up at him. "My father is not as frightening as you may think. But he will insist that we marry in Nottingham before returning back here."

Amelia couldn't contain the joy that filled her chest, reaching out to the tips of her fingers. She would spend the rest of her life in Brighton with Adam. Her heart stung as she remembered Aunt Margaret.

"Will you be staying in Nottingham?" Amelia asked her. She already knew the answer.

"'Tis the only place I belong, my dear. But I will visit Brighton often. I will surely need the cure again next summer."

Amelia would miss her aunt more than she would miss her childhood home, the crowded streets, or even her father.

"You will make a beautiful bride." Aunt Margaret patted Amelia's cheek, blinking fast before turning her face away. Amelia had seen the tears in her eyes. She had not hidden them quickly enough. Amelia slipped her hand from Adam's arm, planting a kiss on her aunt's cheek.

"As will you one day."

Aunt Margaret scoffed, throwing out her hand. "Posh. I have given up on love."

"But there very well may be a man in the world that has not. And you will steal his heart." Amelia shared a glance with Adam before returning her gaze to Aunt Margaret. Her aunt looked at Amelia from under her lashes, intense doubt burning in her expression. She smiled. "I am honored that you believe in me so."

Amelia had learned to believe in many things of late. She believed in the strength of friendship. She believed in the persistence of love. And she believed that fate had sent Eleanor Claridge to Mr. Quinton, and into a secret marriage, all so Amelia and Adam could meet that day at the ocean. She was not certain she believed the cure of the

Brighton waters, but she believed the hope it brought her aunt to be a very good thing, indeed.

The next morning, before the carriage could arrive to convey them to Nottingham, Adam and Amelia walked to the sand of the beach, hand in hand. The sun had cut through the dark clouds, sparkling upon the surface of the sea like thousands of tiny diamonds. She laughed until her stomach ached as Adam told her story after story from his childhood. She would never grow tired of hearing his voice, or being by his side. Her heart had never felt so whole.

In the distance, a bathing machine bobbed upon the waves, a familiar robust woman in the water beside it. The dipper waved, and Amelia remembered the thirty dips she had been given to cure her broken heart. A shiver ran over her spine as she clung to Adam's arm.

"What is the matter?" He followed her gaze to the place the dipper stood in the water.

"The cure is real."

Adam chuckled, stepping around to stand in front of her. "Are you feeling well?"

She gasped when she saw the disbelief in his eyes. "You must possess an open mind, do you remember?"

"I could never believe something so ridiculous." He tipped his head down, the blue of his eyes matching the surrounding waters.

Amelia gave a devious smile. "I once said those words in regard to marriage. Perhaps you might take a dip to change your opinion. It may also, what did my aunt once say, cure you of your disagreeable personality?"

Adam threw his head back in laughter before pulling her close. "I think you have been the only effective cure for that."

"Oh dear. I ought to never leave your side. I should hate for the world to suffer such a disagreeable man again."

He kissed her cheek. "How fortunate I will be to have you as my wife then."

With a full heart, Amelia smiled up at him. She bid a silent farewell to the ocean, to the clear blue sky and the dipper out in the water. For the next time she returned here to Brighton, she would be Mrs. Adam Claridge.

Epilogue

"The water is so cold!" Amelia half laughed, half screeched as she pulled Adam by the hand into the shallow waves of the Brighton waters.

He smiled before bending over to skim the water with his other hand. "Come now, it isn't that cold."

"Yes, it is." Amelia eyed him, a devious smile tugging at her lips.

"No, it's--"

Adam's words stopped as Amelia scooped a handful of water, throwing it at his face. He sputtered in shock before releasing her hand, advancing on her in the water as droplets cascaded down his face.

Amelia shrieked, covering her eyes. The water only reached her ankles here, but the hem of her dress would soon be completely submerged. It was the first day she and Adam had returned to Brighton after their wedding, and in the three weeks of their absence, Amelia had missed the beautiful waters. Her suggestion that they take an evening walk on the beach had not been intended to turn into a war.

Her shoulders tensed, waiting for the freezing water to meet her skin. Instead she felt two strong arms, one behind her knees, the other around her waist, scooping her up. She opened her eyes to see Adam's face only inches from hers, tiny drops of water balanced in his lashes, rolling down the sides of his face. She laughed as he held her suspended above the water.

"What ails you, my dear?"

She shook her head fast, unable to control her giggles. "Nothing!"

Adam laughed, a wicked grin on his lips, taking a step deeper into the water.

"Put me down this instant, Adam Claridge." Amelia peered over his arm that held her suspended. The water was getting closer to her as Adam walked farther into the ocean. She kicked her legs, trying to free herself.

"There must be something that you suffer from," he said, lowering her closer to the surface.

She wrapped her arms tightly around his neck, refusing to let go. Her laughter verged on hysterical. "Yes! I suffer from an intolerable husband that means to drop me in freezing water!"

He chuckled, lowering her an inch from the water before lifting her up again. "I believe throwing water at your husband's face has earned you thirty dips."

"No!"

"No? Would you prefer forty?"

Amelia could almost feel the frigid water soaking into her dress. She froze. It was not her imagination. The water touched her back, sending shivers over her arms. Her stomach hurt from the laughter that shook her. She knew she was guilty. She should have known Adam would seek his revenge. But surely he was only taunting her. Or was he not? His eyes sparked with mischief.

Amelia squeezed her eyes shut, listening to the sound of Adam's deep chuckle and the shifting of the water around her. She ordered herself to think of happy things as a distraction from the cold water that was soon to envelop her. She thought of her wedding gown, the beautiful white that it had been. She thought of her new home in Brighton, and the beautiful town she would never have to leave behind. She thought of her husband, wicked as he was, and how much she adored him still.

Several seconds passed and Amelia was still dry. She opened one eye. Adam tipped his head closer to hers, pressing a kiss to her forehead. "Fortunately for you, stepping in these waters has cured me of my inclination to drop you."

Amelia laughed in relief as he set her down where the water only reached her ankles. She lifted her skirts, venturing deeper into the water. "You believe in the cure now, do you? I never thought it possible." She glanced at him over her shoulder as he followed her.

Adam raised one eyebrow at her. "You are right, it is not possible."

Her eyes widened.

"My inclination to drop you in the water will never be cured."

She shrieked as he wrapped one arm around her waist from behind, pulling her along as he plunged deeper into the ocean. Together they fell backward, sinking into the waist-deep water. Amelia gasped as the bitter temperature engulfed her. She managed to keep her head above the water, but Adam lost his balance, sinking completely below the surface. He burst out of the water, laughing at the scowl on Amelia's face.

She splashed him again, lifting her soaked skirts before running away to the dry sand. She stopped, squeezing the water out of her dress.

Adam trudged out of the ocean, soaked to the bone. Amelia covered her smile.

"Do you still think the water isn't cold?"

He laughed, meeting her on the sand. He picked up his dry jacket from the ground beside her. "It's nothing a warm fire cannot mend," he said, draping the jacket over her shoulders.

Amelia wrapped it around herself, cocooned in warmth from the jacket and the smile in Adam's eyes. The sun had just begun to fall below the horizon, painting the sky in faint streaks of orange and pink.

Together they walked back to their home, laughing until they could scarcely breathe as they talked. The only thing missing was Aunt Margaret, and Amelia eagerly awaited the next summer when her aunt would join them in Brighton once again.

Amelia never could have imagined her trip to Brighton to bring so much change to her life, but she treasured that change. Her entire life had been altered. Her opinions had changed, and her heart had been changed by Adam Claridge. The Brighton waters had not been strong enough to cure her stubborn heart--only Adam had been able to do that.

Amelia held his arm, resting her head against his shoulder as they walked. He kissed the top of her head, drops of water from his hair falling down upon her. But she didn't care.

She took a deep breath and smiled. She was finally home.

Find the complete series on Amazon

Brides of Brighton

A CONVENIENT ENGAGEMENT

MARRYING MISS MILTON

ROMANCING LORD RAMSBURY

MISS WESTON'S WAGER

AN UNEXPECTED BRIDE

About the Author

Ashtyn Newbold grew up with a love of stories. When she discovered chick flicks and Jane Austen books in high school, she learned she was a sucker for romantic ones. When not indulging in sweet romantic comedies and regency period novels (and cookies), she writes romantic stories of her own across several genres. Ashtyn also enjoys baking, singing, sewing, and anything that involves creativity and imagination.

www.ashtynnewbold.com

Made in the USA
Middletown, DE
08 March 2023

26394005R00116